*Also by Susan Vreeland
in Large Print:*

What Love Sees

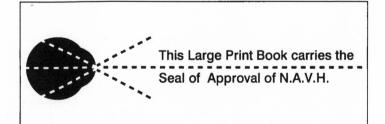
Amazon $28.95 12/10/01

Girl
in Hyacinth Blue

Girl
in Hyacinth Blue

Susan Vreeland

Thorndike Press • Thorndike, Maine

Published in 2000 by arrangement with MacMurray & Beck

Thorndike Large Print ® Basic Series.

The tree indicium is a trademark of Thorndike Press.

The text of this Large Print edition is unabridged.
Other aspects of the book may vary from the original edition.

Set in 16 pt. Plantin.

Printed in the United States on permanent paper.

ISBN 0-7862-2440-1

For Scott Godfrey, D.O.,
and Peter Falk, M.D.

12/01

Acknowledgments

"Love Enough" was originally published under the title "Love Burning" in *New England Review*, "A Night Different From All Other Nights" in *The Missouri Review*, "Morningshine" in *So to Speak*, and "Magdalena Looking" in *Confrontation*.

The author wishes to thank Barbara Braun, Greg Michalson, Fred Ramey, C. Jerry Hannah, and the Asilomar Writers Consortium.

Contents

Thou still unravished bride of quietness
Thou foster-child of Silence and
  slow Time . . .
Thou, silent form! dost tease us
  out of thought
As doth eternity.
                    — John Keats, 1819

Love Enough

Cornelius Engelbrecht invented himself. Let me emphasize, straight away, that he isn't what I would call a friend, but I know him enough to say that he did purposely design himself: single, modest dresser in receding colors, mathematics teacher, sponsor of the chess club, mild-mannered acquaintance to all rather than a friend to any, a person anxious to become invisible. However, that exterior blandness masked a burning center, and for some reason that became clear to me only later, Cornelius Engelbrecht revealed to me the secret obsession that lay beneath his orderly, controlled design.

It was after Dean Merrill's funeral that I began to see Cornelius's unmasked heart. We'd all felt the shock of Merrill's sudden death, a loss that thrust us into a temporary intimacy uncommon in the faculty lunchroom of our small private boys' academy, but it wasn't shock or Cornelius's head start in drinking that snowy afternoon in Penn's Den where we'd gone after the funeral that made him forsake his strategy of obscurity. Someone at the table remarked about Merrill's cryptic last words, "love enough," words that now sting me as much as any indictment of my complicity or encouragement, but they didn't then. We began talking of last words of famous people and of our dead relatives, and Cornelius dipped his head and fastened his gaze on his dark beer. I only noticed because chance had placed us next to each other at the table.

He spoke to his beer rather than to any of us. " 'An eye like a blue pearl,' was what my father said. And then he died. During a winter's first snowfall, just like this."

Cornelius had a face I'd always associated with Piero della Francesca's portrait of the Duke of Urbino. It was the shape of his nose, narrow but extremely high-bridged, providing a bench for glasses he did not wear. He seemed a man distracted by a mystery or preoccupied by an intellectual or moral dilemma so consuming that it made him feel superior, above those of us whose concerns were tires for the car or a child's flu. Whenever our talk moved toward the mundane, he became distant, as though he were mulling over something far more weighty, which made his cool smiles patronizing.

"Eye like a blue pearl? What's that mean?" I asked.

He studied my face as if measuring me against some private criteria. "I can't explain it, Richard, but I might show you."

In fact, he insisted that I come to his home that evening, which was entirely out of character. I'd never seen him insist on anything. It would call attention to himself. I think Merrill's "love enough" had somehow stirred him, or else he thought it might stir me. As I say, why he picked me I couldn't tell, unless it was simply that I was the only artist or art teacher he knew.

He took me down a hallway into a spacious study piled with books, the door curiously locked even though he lived alone. Closed off, the room was chilly so he lit a fire. "I don't usually have guests," he explained, and directed me to sit in the one easy chair, plum-colored leather, high-backed and expensive, next to the fireplace and opposite a painting. A most extraordinary painting in which a young girl wearing a short blue smock over a rust-colored skirt sat in profile at a table by an open window.

"My God," I said. It must have been what he'd wanted to hear, for it unleashed a

11

string of directives, delivered at high pitch.

"Look. Look at her eye. Like a pearl. Pearls were favorite items of Vermeer. The longing in her expression. And look at that Delft light spilling onto her forehead from the window." He took out his handkerchief and, careful not to touch the painting, wiped the frame, though I saw no dust at all. "See here," he said, "the grace of her hand, idle, palm up. How he consecrated a single moment in that hand. But more than that —"

"Remarkable," I said. "Certainly done in the style of Vermeer. A beguiling imitation."

Cornelius placed his hands on the arm of the chair and leaned toward me until I felt his breath on my forehead. "It is a Vermeer," he whispered.

I sputtered at the thought, the absurdity, his belief. "There were many done in the style of Vermeer, and of Rembrandt. School of Rubens, and the like. The art world is full of copyists."

"It is a Vermeer," he said again. The solemnity of his tone drew my eyes from the painting to him. He appeared to be biting the inside of his cheek. "You don't think so?" he asked, his hand going up to cover his heart.

"It's just that there are so few." I hated to disillusion the man.

"Yes, surely, very few. Very few. He did at the most forty canvases. And only a matter of thirty to thirty-five are located. *Welk een schat! En waar is dat alles gebleven?*"

"What's that?"

"Just the lament of some Dutch art historian. Where has such a treasure gone, or some such thing." He turned to pour us both a brandy. "So why could this not be? It's his same window opening inward at the left that he used so often, the same splash of pale yellow light. Take a look at the figures in the tapestry on the table. Same as in nine other paintings. Same Spanish chair with lion's head finials that he used in eleven canvases, same brass studs in the leather. Same black and white tiles placed diagonally on the floor."

"Subject matter alone does not prove authenticity."

"Granted, but I take you to be a man of keen observation. You are an artist, Richard. Surely you can see that the floor suffers the same distortion of tiles he had in his earlier work, for example, *The Music Lesson*, roughly dated 1662 to '64, or *Girl with the Wineglass*, 1660."

I never would have guessed he knew all

this. He reeled it off like a textbook. Well, so could I. "That can likewise prove it was done by an inferior imitator, or by van Mieris, or de Hooch. They all did tile floors. Holland was paved with tile."

"Yes, yes, I know. Even George III thought *The Music Lesson* was a van Mieris when he bought it, but even a king can't make it so. It's a Vermeer." He whispered the name.

I hardly knew what to say. It was too implausible.

He cleared off books and papers from the corner of his large oak desk, propped himself there and leaned toward me. "I can see you still doubt. Study, if you will, the varying depths of field. Take a look at the sewing basket placed forward on the table, as he often did, by the way, almost as an obstruction between the viewer and the figure. Its weave is diffused, slightly out of focus, yet the girl's face is sharply in focus. Look at the lace edge of her cap. Absolutely precise to a pinprick right there at her temple. And now look at the glass of milk. Soft-edged, and the map on the wall only a suggestion. Agreed?"

I nodded, more out of regard for his urgency than in accord.

"Well, then, he did the same in *The*

Lacemaker, 1669. Which leads me to surmise this was done between 1665 and 1668."

I felt his eyes boring into me as I examined the painting. "You've amassed a great deal of information. Is there a signature?"

"No, no signature. But that was not unusual. He often failed to sign his work. Besides, he had at least seven styles of signature. For Vermeer, signatures are not definite evidence. Technique is. Look at the direction of the brush's stroke, those tiny grooves of the brush hairs. They have their lighted and their shaded side. Look elsewhere. You'll find overlapping layers of paint no thicker than silk thread that give a minute difference in shade. That's what makes it a Vermeer."

I walked toward the painting, took off my glasses to see that close, and it was as he had said. If I moved my head to the right or left, certain brush strokes subtly changed their tint. How difficult it was to achieve that. In other places the surface was so smooth the color must have floated onto the canvas. I suddenly found myself breathing fast. "Haven't you had it appraised? I know an art history professor who could come and have a look."

"No, no. I prefer it not be known. Security risks. I just wanted you to see it, because you can appreciate it. Don't tell a soul, Richard."

"But if it were validated by authorities . . . why, the value would be astronomical. A newly discovered Vermeer — it would rock the art world."

"I don't want to rock the art world." The blood vessel in his temple pulsated, whether out of conviction of the painting's authenticity or something else, I didn't know.

"Forgive my indelicacy, but how did you obtain it?"

He fixed on me a stony look. "My father, who always had a quick eye for fine art, picked it up, let us say, at an advantageous moment."

"An estate sale or an auction? Then there'd be papers."

"No. No Vermeer has been auctioned since World War I. Let's just say it was privately obtained. By my father, who gave it to me when he died." The line of his jaw hardened. "So there are no records, if that's what you're thinking. And no bill of sale." His voice had a queer defiance.

"The provenance?"

"There are several possibilities. Most of Vermeer's work passed through the hands

16

of one Pieter Claesz van Ruijven, son of a wealthy Delft brewer. I believe this one did not. When Vermeer died, he left his wife with eleven children and a drawerful of debts. Five hundred guilders for groceries. Another sum for woolens for which the merchant Jannetje Stevens seized twenty-six paintings. Later they were negotiated back to the widow, but only twenty-one of them were auctioned in the settling of his estate. Who got the other five? Artists or dealers in the Guild of St. Luke? Neighbors? Family? This could be one. And of those twenty-one, only sixteen have been identified. Where did the others go? A possibility there too. Also, a baker, Hendrick van Buyten, held two as collateral against a bread bill of six hundred seventeen guilders. Some think van Buyten had even obtained a couple others earlier."

I had to be careful not to be taken in. Just because Cornelius knew facts about Vermeer didn't make his painting one.

"Later, it could have been sold as a de Hooch, whose work was more marketable at the time. Or it could have been thrown in as extra *puyk,* a giveaway item in the sale of a collection of de Hooches or van der Werffs, or it could have been in the estate sale of Pieter Tjammens in Groningen."

17

He was beyond me now. What sort of person knew that kind of detail?

"Documents report only 'an auction of curious paintings by important masters such as J. van der Meer that had been kept far away from the capital.' There are plenty of possibilities."

All this spilled out of him in a flood. A math teacher! Unbelievable.

But the question of how Cornelius's father obtained the painting, he deftly avoided. I did not know him well enough to press further without being pushy. Not knowing this which he so carefully kept private, I could not believe it to be genuine. I finished the brandy and extricated myself, politely enough, thinking, so what if it isn't a Vermeer? The painting's exquisite. Let the fellow enjoy it.

His father. Presumably the same name. Engelbrecht. German.

Why was it so vital that I concur? Some great thing must be hanging in the balance.

I drove home, trying to put it all out of my mind, yet the face of the girl remained.

Merrill's funeral the day before had made Cornelius thoughtful. Not of Merrill particularly. Of the unpredictableness of one's end, and what remains unpardoned. And of his father. Snow had blanketed his father's coffin too — specks at first, then connecting, then piling up until the coffin became a white puffy loaf. That jowl-faced minister saying, "One must take notice of the measure of a man" was the only thing said during Merrill's service that he remembered.

Cornelius had to admit on his father's behalf that Otto Engelbrecht was a dutiful father, often stern and then suddenly tender during Cornelius's childhood in Duisburg, near the Dutch border. On this lonely Sunday afternoon with snow still falling gently, Cornelius, reading in his big leather chair, looked up from the page and tried to recall his earliest memory of his father. It may have been his father giving him the little wooden windmill brought back from Holland. It had painted blue blades that turned and a little red door with one hinge missing that opened to reveal a tiny wooden family inside.

He remembered how his father had spent Sunday afternoons with him, the only child — took him to the Dusseldorf Zoo, gave him trumpet lessons himself, pulled him in a sled through the neighborhood, and when Cornelius suffered from the cold, how his father enfolded Cornelius's small hand in his and drew it into his pocket. He taught him chess strategies and made him memorize them, explained in a Dutch museum the reason for van Gogh's tortured skies, the genius of Rembrandt's faces, and when they moved to America, a result of his father's credo to seize advantageous moments, he took him to see the Yankees in Yankee Stadium. These facts Cornelius saw now as only the good intentions of a patched-up life.

Later, in Philadelphia, he was embarrassed by his father's hovering nervousness whenever he brought home a school friend, and understood only vaguely his father's dark command, "If they ask, tell them we are Swiss, and don't say another word." By the time he brought home friends from college, his father had moved the painting into the study and installed a lock, secreting it with a niggard's glee. His father's self-satisfied posture whenever he looked at the painting — hands clasped behind his back, rocking on his toes, then heels — became, for a time, a source of nausea to him.

After his mother died, his father, retired and restless, took over tending her garden. Cornelius remembered now the ardent slope of his shoulders as he stooped to eradicate any deviant weed sprouting between rows of cauliflower and cabbage. Did he have to be so relentless? Couldn't he just let one grow, and say I don't know how it slipped through? Joyfully he planted, watered, gave away grocery sacks of vegetables to neighbors.

"Such wonderful tomatoes," one woman marveled.

"You can't get a decent tomato in the supermarket these days." Smiling, he heaped more in her sack.

"We had a victory garden like this during the war," she said, and Cornelius saw him flinch.

Was that his father's Luger, grown huge in his mind, cracking down on a woman's hand reaching for a bun as she was hurried from her kitchen?

The line between memory and imagination was muddled by years of intense rumination, of horrified reading, one book after another devoured with carnivorous urgency — histories, personal accounts, diaries, documents, war novels — and Cornelius could not be sure now what parts he'd read, what parts he'd overheard his father, Lieutenant Otto Engelbrecht, telling Uncle Friederich about the Raid of the Two Thousand, what became known to academics as Black Thursday, August 6, 1942.

From dark to midnight, they dragged them out of their houses, the raid ordered, historians said, because too few Jews called-up for deportation were reporting at the station, and the train to Westerbork had to be filled. By mid-August they moved to South Amsterdam, a more prosperous area. In September, they were still at it, carting them off to Zentralstelle on van Scheltema Square.

Just like the assembly line at the Duisburg plant. From somewhere, his father's voice.

The rest was a tangle of the printed and the spoken word, enlarged by the workings of his imagination. He played in his mind again the Duisburg memory of creeping back downstairs after bedtime and overhearing his father telling Uncle Friederich the story he, a ten-year-old, didn't understand then. This time he staged it as though his father, after too much Scotch, and bloated by a checkmate following too many losses to Friederich, told his brother when in family circles it was still safe to speak, "You've got to see opportunities and seize them on the spot. That's how it's done. Or, if a quick move isn't expedient, make a plan. Like that painting. When my aide spotted a silver tea set in some Jew's dining room, he made a move to bag it. Wrong time. I had to stop him. Property of the Fuhrer."

Cornelius had read of that, the Puls van following the raids the next day, street by street, to cart away ownerless Jewish possessions for the Hausraterfassung, the Department for the Appropriation of Household Effects.

"That's when I saw that painting, behind his head. All blues and yellows and reddish brown, as translucent as lacquer. It had to be a Dutch master. Just then a private found a little kid covered with tablecloths behind some dishes in a sideboard cabinet. We'd almost missed him. My aide glared at me, full of accusation that I could slip like that and be distracted. With any excuse — the painting, for example, or my reprimand — he might even have reported it."

What always rang in his mind with the crash of dishes, Cornelius would never now be sure was memory or his own swollen imagination: "So I shoved my boot up the Jew-boy's dirty ass. But I took care to note the house number."

What had happened next wasn't difficult

to piece together. As soon as they delivered their quota, at 1:00 or 2:00 A.M., while other Jews still lay frozen in their hiding places and when the streets were dead quiet, his father went back. The painting was still there, hanging in spite of Decree 58/42, reported in several histories: All Jewish art collections had to be deposited with Lippmann and Rosenthal, a holding company. But this was not a collection, only a single painting, blatantly displayed, or ignorantly. What could his father have thought? That therefore it deserved to be taken? And then would come his father's voice resounding somehow through the years, "By the time I got there, the tea set was already gone."

Going over the same visions he thought his father had, hoped his father had, kept Cornelius awake at night, filled his dreams with the orgy of plunder, mothers not chosen lining up to die, pain not linked to sin, smoke drifting across fences and coating windows of Christian homes, children's teeth like burnt pearls. Driven by imagination, he read like a zealot on two subjects: Dutch art and the German occupation of the Netherlands. Only one gave him pleasure. Only one might dissolve the image of his father's hat and boots and Luger.

Compelled by his need to know, Cornelius traveled to Amsterdam one summer. He avoided van Scheltema Square, went straight to the Rijksmuseum, examined breathlessly Vermeer's works, and in one delicious afternoon, convinced himself of the authenticity of his family's prize by seeing layers of thin paint applied in grooved brush strokes creating light and shadow on the blue sleeve of a lady reading a letter, just like those on the sleeve of his sewing girl. A few days later he went to The Hague. At the Royal Cabinet of Paintings in the Mauritshuis, he saw points of brilliant pink-white light at the corners of the opened mouth and in the eyes of Vermeer's girl in a red feathered hat, the same as on his sewing girl. In the musty municipal archives of Delft, Amsterdam, Leiden and Groningen he poured through old documents and accounts of estate sales. He found only possibilities, no undeniable evidence. Still, the evidence was in the museums — the similarities were undeniable. He flew home, hoarding conviction like a stolen jewel.

"It is. It is," he told his father.

Then came the slow smile that cracked his father's face. "I knew it had to be."

Together they went over every square inch of the painting, seduced anew by its charms, yet the rapture was insufficient to drown out the truth Cornelius could no longer deny: If the painting were real, so was the atrocity of his father's looting. He'd had no other way to obtain it. Now with Friederich and his mother gone, only two in the whole world knew, and that, together with the twin images in their dreams, bound them willingly or not into a double kinship.

He started to tell someone else once, his one-time wife who had laughed when he said it was a Vermeer. Laughed, and asked how his father got it, and he couldn't say, and her laughter jangled in his ears long afterward. She claimed he turned cold to her after that, and within a year she left, saying he loved things rather than people. The possible truth of the accusation haunted him with all the rest.

After his father's stroke, when the money from such a painting would set him up finely in a rest home, Cornelius agonized. Even an inquiry to a dealer might bring Israeli agents to his father's door with guns and extradition papers efficiently negotiated by the internationally operating Jewish Documentation Center, and a one-way plane ticket to Jerusalem, courtesy of the Mossad. More than a thousand had been hunted down so far, and not just Reichskommissars or SS Commandants either, so Cornelius moved back home to care for him.

Finally, when there would be no more afternoons of wheeling him, freshly bathed and shaven, out to the sun of the garden, when pain clutched through the drugs, his father murmured fragments, in German, the language he'd left behind. In a room soured by the smell of dying, a smell Cornelius knew his father could recognize, Otto whispered, "Bring the painting in."

When they both knew the end was close, Cornelius heard, faintly, "I only joined because of the opportunity to make life-long friendships with people on the rise."

Cornelius sniggered, then spooned crushed ice between his father's parched lips.

"I only saw the trains. That's all I knew."

He wiped with a tissue a dribble inching down his father's chin, and waited for his father's breath, suspended in indecision, to come again.

"No more than forwarding agents. Sending them from one address to another. What happened at the other end was none of my business."

Right. Of course. This way for the trains, please. Careful, madam. Watch your step. Coolly Cornelius watched a pain worm across his father's forehead. How had he deserved to live so long?

"The thought of opposing or evading orders never entered my head."

Precisely.

Like a moulting snake, Cornelius thought, his father made pathetic efforts to shed the skin of sin in order to get down to the marrow of his innocence in time. But on the last morning, with opaque gray snow fog closing in, came the truth of his grief: "I never reached a high rank."

That allowed Cornelius to bury him inexpensively. Without notice. It wasn't a cruel thing, he told himself. Call it a memorial act, aimed at cheating the world of its triumph by ignominy, but by its very privacy, it failed. He did his best, that is, while his father was still living, did what he could, what he could pry out of himself. Nobody could say he didn't. Alone in this same study, sitting in his father's leather chair that struck him now as being the color of a bruise, he'd read the will. He'd forced his eyes to register each line and not scan down the page to see what he knew he'd see, that "a painting of a young girl sewing at a window" was his.

Now, for good or ill, there it hung. He felt its presence whenever he came into the room.

On this silent Sunday afternoon, years after his father's quiet burial, and the day after Merrill's, Cornelius sat in the same study, his now, reading Eichmann's trial records and drinking rum and coffee. Outside his window snow was flattening what had been his father's garden, and across the city it was pressing down on the new grave of Dean Merrill and the small boy's wooden sacrifice. Inside, he looked up, saw the life in the girl's eyes, and wished — no, longed for someone, Richard, anyone to enjoy the painting with him. No, not just anyone. Richard was safe. He knew art but not art dealers. That old wild need rumbled up from some molten place within, that need to say, "Look at this stupendous achievement. Look at this Vermeer. Pay attention on your knees to greatness."

At least he'd had that with his father. Once, years earlier, his father had called him long distance when he discovered what he thought was a brush hair left in a mullion of the window. That hair, from Vermeer's own brush, ah! He should have shown it to Richard. To dissolve his doubt. Once he believed, Richard would have the passion to enjoy it like his father had.

His eyes fell to the page and stuck on a line said by Eichmann's judge: "The process of extermination was a single, all embracing operation, and cannot be divided into individual deeds." No. He didn't agree. He thought of the nameless, graveless little boy kicked out the door who may have played with a wooden toy his last free morning in the world.

Did the toy windmill get appropriated too? A souvenir from some hapless Jewish home taken at an advantageous moment in spite of its missing hinge? He imagined his father encased in a glass booth, being interrogated: "And did you not remove this windmill from the house at 72 Rijnstraat after breaking in on the night of 3 September, 1942?" His own third birthday.

Willed or not, the painting didn't belong to him.

It would be doing penance for his father if he himself wouldn't enjoy it more. He tore newspaper into strips, fanned them out and crumpled them over the grate. Then the kindling, crosswise, then the quartered logs. The fireplace opening was barely wide enough. He was grateful it

ued as cruel or rigid or
now this boiling need
rack the eggshell of his
structed self. The one
to be believed, struck at
ng he most feared, to be
with his century's supreme
e to risk exposure for the
delighting with another,
er was gone, in the lumi-
eye. To delight for a day,
himself. A promise.
ll did not believe. He had
ore saying, "Whether it's
meer or not, it is a mar-
Marvelous painting, mar-
That was not enough.
reds of marvelous paint-
y. This was a *Vermeer*.
m Richard would satisfy.
ome authentic reason for
The possibility of illegiti-
'd suffered for was like a
he power to waken him
t the dream gripped hard,
awakened, crying child,
t give it up.
lmired the work. He was,
rush hair's breadth away
The relief from sharing

wasn't a large painting; it would be a shame to do it injury with a razor.

He stood up to lift the painting off the wall. This one last afternoon, he would allow himself a luxury he'd never permitted himself before: He touched her cheek. A quiver ran through his body as the age cracks passed beneath the pads of his fingertips. He stroked her neck and was surprised he could not grasp the tie string hanging from her cap. And then her shoulder, and he was astonished he could not feel its roundness. She hardly had breasts. He moistened his lips suddenly gone dry, and touched there too, more delicately, two fingers only, and felt himself give in to a great wave of embarrassed and awkward pity, as when one glances in a hospital doorway at a person partially naked.

Where her skirt gathered, he felt the grooves left by Jan's brush. Jan. Johannes. No. Jan. The familiar name the only appropriate one for a moment like this. Jan's brush. He thought perhaps his fingers were too rough to feel Jan's mastery. He went to the bathroom, shaved with a new razor, dried his face carefully, and, back in his study leaning toward the wall, he placed his cheek next to her dress. The shock of its coldness knifed through him.

He had no right to this.

He laid the painting on the carpet and lit the fire. Kneeling, waiting for the flames to catch, he imagined them creeping toward the pale blue pearl of her eye. The quiet intensity of her longing stilled his hand a moment more.

If he turned the painting over, maybe he could do it.

Such an act of selfishness, he thought, to destroy for personal peace what rightly belonged to the world at large, a piece of the mosaic of the world's fine art. That would be an act equally cruel as any of his father's.

No. Nothing would be. Not just his father's looting — the safe job of thievery behind the battle lines — not just his father's routing them out, but the whole connected web. In Eichmann's trial record, he'd read, "The legal responsibility of those who deliver the victim to his death is, in our eyes, no less than that of those who kill the victim," and he'd agreed.

Now, waiting for the fullness of the flame, it occurred to him, if the painting wasn't authentically a Vermeer — after all, he had no solid proof — he could do it, couldn't he? He could burn the thing, put

with one person who did not laugh was intoxicating. Why he didn't do it years ago, he couldn't say. He'd wasted years in a miser's clutch, protecting a father who had protected no one. He wanted more. For the first time, he imagined himself telling it all, the history and his father's part of it, so Richard would believe, telling it with burning eyes right there in front of the painting, and he would not die. He would not die from shame.

He kept repeating it — *I will not die* — while the flames burnt down to coals.

The painting bound me to Cornelius with a curious tie, compelling but misbegotten, so that when I saw him mornings at the faculty mail room, the thought of that strange, secretive evening and his perverse insistence troubled me still. I felt I'd been plucked by the sleeve and commanded to follow him into a dangerous sea of judgment that could rise up against me as well.

We kept a coded language. One day I asked, not to goad him, but strictly as an aesthetics issue, "Would you enjoy it any less if you were to learn it wasn't authentic?"

"But it is."

"Yes, but just supposing it weren't?"

"I don't have to think about that. I know."

His bloated sureness irritated me.

I had the distinct impression that he was not at home in the world, and I knew it had to do with that painting. I did a bit of reading, talked to my art historian friend, and one Friday afternoon in the parking lot at school I asked him, "Did you know that a Dutch painter named van Meergeren forged some Vermeers in the 1930s?" He froze there by his car. "So real he had the art critics and curators believing him?"

"Yes, I was aware of that." Cornelius straightened up stiffly.

"And you know how they found out? He sold a few to that Nazi, Goering, and the Dutch government arrested him for treason — collaborating with the enemy, letting Dutch masters leak out of Holland into the hands of the Reichstag. And so he confessed."

Cornelius's eyes darted back to his car where his hand trembled trying to find the keyhole. In that quiver I knew I had inadvertently stumbled onto something. Maybe he knew it was only a van Meergeren all along, and was trying to make a dupe of me, or sell it to me for an exorbitant price. A friend might let it pass, but we were only colleagues, committed, both of us, the mathematician and the artist, to truth. "I'd like to see it again, if you wouldn't mind," I said.

"Whenever you'd like," he said, all cordiality, and made a move to get into his car.

"How about now?"

He stood still a moment, gathering himself, it seemed to me. "No time like the present."

In the daylight the painting was even more magnificent than I remembered it. I sank into the chair in a trance. The luster of the glass of milk shining like the surface of a pearl made me believe — this was no copyist's art — but Cornelius's puffed-up manner the weeks before made me obstinate.

Yet now he had none of that smugness. There was only the intense pleasure of the painting. Lovingly he poured over its surface with an intimacy I hadn't noticed before in his flood of facts. If ever a man loved a work of art, it was Cornelius. His face shone with the adoration of a pilgrim for the icon of his God.

"I'd like to believe. It's not that I want to kill your own belief. But there's still one huge question."

"Which is?"

"Cornelius, you and I are teachers. Our fathers weren't millionaires. Unless you tell me how he obtained it, I don't see how —"

The radiance drained from his face.

I let the suggestion lie there and took a sip of the beer he'd brought me. He finished his in one long, thoughtful draft, and held on to the bottle after he'd set it down, as if to anchor himself. I waited.

"I grew up in Duisburg, near the Dutch border . . . ," he began, keeping his gaze riveted to the young girl while he spoke of his childhood, as though ingesting strength from her calm.

"And here, after sweating through a high school history class, I asked in spite of Mother's solemn warning never to ask, 'What did you do in the war, Dad?' 'Worked in Amsterdam,' was all he said. Just like it was a job. 'Yes, but what did you do?' I asked. 'I have a right to know.' His body stopped all motion even out to his fingertips, as if he were feeling the first tremors of an earthquake. 'Took them to the trains,' he said."

Cornelius turned to me then.

"He took me to Yankee Stadium. Kept my hand warm in his own pocket. Planted daffodils for my mother. If I could have wept, if he had not trained it out of me . . . after that, he never was the same to me."

Cornelius's eyes, when he told me of the boy in the cabinet, became glazed like melted glass, and there was a hardness to his voice when he told of the missing tea set. When he said he'd tried to burn the painting, his whole body shook, and he slumped down at his desk, spent.

Worse, a hundred times worse than I'd thought. That he had tried to destroy it, I could hardly believe. That he thought such an act might atone sickened me. I did not, I was sorry to learn, find in myself any generosity or charitableness for this man in spite of his suffering.

Clutching the edge of his desk with both hands, he leaned toward me, his forehead a torture of grooves above that hook of a nose. "You won't tell, will you, the others at school? You see, now that you . . . now that one person in the world sees that it's authentic, it's all worthwhile, don't you think?"

His upper lip twitched in a repulsive way as though tugged by a thread. It became clear to me then why he picked me. He thought an artist might excuse, out of awe for the work, and if I excused, the painting could live.

"What happened to the boy?"

He stammered a moment, unable to put into words what we both knew.

"You know what they say, Cornelius. One good burning deserves another."

I left him hunched there, took another look at the painting I knew would be my last, and could not get out of there fast enough. Poor fool, ruining his life for a piece of cloth smeared with mineral paste, for a fake, I had to tell myself, a mere curiosity.

With that to do ahead of him now, how he'd face me, how I'd face him Monday morning, I didn't know.

A Night Different From All Other Nights

The day before, Hannah Vredenburg and her younger brother Tobias watched their father let his partner's pigeons go, back to their home in Antwerp. One by one, waiting between each for safety, he released them from the attic coop when the early morning was still foggy so no passing officer might see and note the house number. The decree against Amsterdam Jews keeping pigeons — their own or somebody else's — was eight months old, and Hannah knew it was getting too dangerous to disobey. Surrendering them this late at the German police station, as the decree had ordered, would result in repercussions.

"Quickly, Hannah, before Tobias comes up," her father had said, and handed her the paper and pencil in hands trembling too much to write. "Here, write this. Write small." It was the message to be placed in the tiny canister of his partner's last bird.

41

"Kill my pigeons," he whispered, pausing between sentences. "I can't expect you to feed them for the duration. Don't endanger yourself and don't release them, but let them eat their fill first. Leo with the purple-edged wings likes lentils best. Henriette, the blue-barred female, likes to have her head rubbed. This will be the last message until it's over, God willing. We are well. May you be safe."

That last! Even as she squeezed those last four words onto the little paper, Hannah felt a frantic fluttering against the inside of her rib cage.

"Do I sign your name?"

"No."

She folded the paper just as Tobias came up the ladder in his pajamas.

One by one Father scooped up his partner's pigeons, held them gently so Tobias could stroke them one last time, cupped his hands under their breasts and swung his arms upward to launch them into the air. She handed Father the folded message, which he slipped into the canister of the last bird. She watched him kiss the back of the bird's head, a small moment with closed eyes, and then he flung the last pigeon skyward.

She watched that last free flapping of

wings as the bird rose over the peaked roofs to his home in Antwerp. Escape that was no escape. Antwerp, Amsterdam — what difference did it make?

The next day, coming home from school, she saw Henriette, Leo and their two others fly under the gable and peck around the roof trying to get into their own home coop. She felt her breath leak out and leave only blackness: The message got there too late. Her father's partner had already released her family's own pigeons. She hurried inside, up the ladder stairs and let them in the coop. Their messages told of the German takeover of the diamond trade in Antwerp. A chill spread over her fingers and up her throat as she removed the canisters. She knew at once what must be done. It was only a matter of time. How long before Tobias would realize it too?

That night she stood on the ladder looking into the attic coop while her father, crosslegged on the coop floor, crooned to his birds, and to Tobias. "Leo. Leo. Such a bird. A bird that could carry a two-carat stone in his canister and never feel the weight. Remember that faithfulness, Toby."

She cried then, holding tight to the top rung of the ladder so she wouldn't make a sound. Father's words might tell Tobias what had to be done. He wouldn't be told to remember Leo if Leo could live. She watched Tobias search Father's face a moment. Then he went back to stroking the gray breast feathers of the pigeons, feeding them barley out of his palm. But he didn't giggle as he usually did when Leo's rose-colored toes tickled his arm. She crept back downstairs.

It was awful they couldn't just be freed. That would be fitting to do on Passover, but they'd be bewildered by freedom, she thought, frightened of the prospects of finding a speck of food in South Amsterdam. They'd only peck around the gable of the house to get back into the coop. It would make it obvious that this was the house where they belonged.

The next morning at breakfast, she asked, "Will it be today?"

"Soon." Father gently placed his big palm on the back of her head for a moment.

The whole house waited, breathless, while Passover approached, the night different from all other nights. Mother and Grandmother Hilde had been cleaning kitchen cabinets, the pantry, the oven, the icebox, and now were cleaning shelves in the sideboard and putting away the silver tea set in order to make room on the top for the Passover china. Hannah sat looking at the painting above the sideboard. It was of a girl her own age looking out a window while sewing. The way she leaned forward, intent on something, and the longing in her eyes cast a spell over her every time she looked. The girl wasn't working, at least not at that moment. Her hands were lax, the buttons on the table like flat pearls yet to be sewn on, because what was going on in her mind was more important. Hannah understood that.

It was on an excursion with Father, just the two of them, a couple years earlier that he bought the painting — 1940, just before her eleventh birthday. He'd been going to meetings of the Comite voor Joodsche Vluchtelingen, Jewish refugees from Germany, in the Rotterdam Cafe next to the Diamond Exchange and had taken her to an auction where families had donated paintings, vases, jewelry and Oriental rugs to be bid on by other families as a means to raise money for refugee support. It was essential, he'd said, that the government not bear the expense of the Jewish poor. When this painting came up for bid, she gasped. The face of the girl in the painting almost glowed, her blue eyes, cheeks, the corners of her mouth all bright and glossy, the light coming right at her across the space between them. She seemed more real than the people in the room.

When Father cast a bid, Hannah sucked in her breath, astonished. He bid again. He grasped her hand when the bidding got above two hundred guilders; she squeezed his back when it passed three hundred. The higher the bids, the tighter she squeezed until, when he cast the bid that bought it, she cried, "Papa!" and didn't let go of his hand all the way home. Father buying it seemed to honor her in a way that made her feel worthy.

The moment they walked in with the painting, while it was still wrapped, Mother straightened up and looked from her to Father as if she could tell something significant had happened. Hannah remembered feeling light-headed as she walked through the rooms choosing a place, until she settled on the dining room above the sideboard. She unwrapped it and held it up. "See Mamela, how lovely?" Sitting bolt upright across from it at the dining table, just where she was sitting now, she was the last to go to bed that night.

Tobias came in through the front vestibule. "Hannah, isn't this interesting?" He had in his hand a new spring leaf. "On this edge there are twenty-four spikes but only twenty-two on this," he said. "Why?"

At nine years old, Tobias was full of questions. He loved spider webs and the sound of crickets, kept moth and beetle collections, a small green turtle, a rabbit named Elijah, a notebook where he drew his observations from nature. In his mind, the four years between them made her ultimately knowledgeable, but she never knew what to say. She couldn't answer his passion with hers. "I don't know, Toby. Some things are different, I suppose."

Just then Mother asked him to clean the coop of *hametz,* which meant all barley, peas, lentils, any grain that would leaven when moist. Ridding the house of leavening was an act of remembrance, for Passover. Mother gave him only a couple dried potato peelings as alternate food for the birds since she used those in soup nowadays.

In the momentary silence, hearing only the coos of the pigeons echoing down the open air vent and her mother's damp cloth whooshing across a shelf, Hannah watched bewilderment descend on Toby's face. He stared at the peelings in his hand, then looked up at her.

"What are they going to eat tomorrow?" he asked.

It was another question she couldn't answer.

His eyes darkened, his smooth forehead furrowed, and for a moment she imagined him, impossibly, as an old man. He knows it's only a token, she thought. If he didn't want to see them suffer, it would have to be done quickly. She saw confusion weight his shoulders and slick over his eyes. She reached out to put her arm around him. He drew away. Sobbing, he flung himself down the hallway and clambered up the ladder to the attic coop. She felt some nameless thing clutch at her heart.

As soon as he left, Hilde said to Mother, "It's terrible to make a child cry so." Whenever someone left the room, Hilde always had something to say about the person. Hilde drummed her fingernails on the sideboard for emphasis. "Let Hannah clean the coop."

"He loves those birds, Hilde. Let him be with them. Let him grieve. This year he'll understand the Passover story."

Mother fairly attacked the sideboard shelves. In fact, she seemed to scrub everything more ferociously this year. Unbelievable that somehow she continued to clean.

Sputtering, Hilde swung around at Hannah. "Why don't you help your mother?"

Hannah shrugged and dangled a crumple of paper on a string in front of Toby's cat. The boiling of the silverware, the cleaning of the kitchen, the cooking, none of it interested her now.

"That's not an answer."

"I don't want to."

"Want to, she says. What's to want? You just do."

"Everybody does a little, Hannah," her mother said. "Won't you help boil the utensils?"

"Everybody works," Hilde said. "That's what life is. Work and a little play and a lot of prayer. Your great-grandmother Etty worked on the drivewheel you know. Walked the crank in a circle for thirty years until she wore a groove in the floor to power her husband's polishing scaife. She worked without a complaint until 1867 when she was —"

"Replaced by a horse. I know. You told me the last time you came."

"Well? Helping your mother is nothing compared to that. You want to be married, don't you? You've got to learn how to do these things. Or do you want to end up an old maid working in a sweatshop? Edith tells me you don't do your lessons either. That you don't like school. Unthinkable. You want to go back to the crank?"

Hannah shrugged again. It might not be so bad. If nobody pestered her.

"What do you think we've worked hard all these years for, so you can become a cigar maker? A peddler? That's what happens, you know, to Jews who don't work hard."

Hannah looked at Hilde's gray wool bedroom scuffs aimed at her like two tail-less rats.

"First generation your father is, to be a diamond merchant and not a polisher. That doesn't mean something to you?"

Out of the corner of her eye Hannah saw her mother cringe. "Will you at least go to the grocer for the parsley and the egg?" Mother asked. "Sal Meyer is saving a shank bone for me. It's a lovely day out. The lime trees along Scheldestraat must have new spring leaves by now. Brush your hair and go."

Without a word Hannah put on her unraveling maroon sweater with the stiff new star, but she moved so slowly after Mother gave her the money that Hilde raised up in righteous outrage, her glare passing from Hannah to Mother and back again. For a second, she dared glare back before she stepped into the vestibule and left the door open a crack to listen.

Hilde waited only a few seconds. "That girl! She never works. She never talks. Can't you get her to talk?"

"How to make her talk. Tell me. I'm sure you know."

"She has no interests. No friends. Last night I asked what she'd been doing this winter and she said 'nothing.' Does she even think?"

"Hilde, don't be cruel. We may never know what she's thinking, but surely she does."

"You should get her to participate."

"You think because I am her mother I can remake her? You're her grandmother. You have a try. She is what she is."

"Lazy and apathetic."

"I suppose when you were her age you never felt like you just wanted to sit and think? You think I don't already ask myself before sleep mercifully takes me what I did or didn't do that made her this way? What I failed to say to her at one unknown, privately crucial day? Tell me, Hilde, how haven't I loved enough? Tell me."

Hannah couldn't breathe. She peeled paint off the woodwork around the inner door.

"All I know, Edith, is that you've got to do something or she won't have the strength. Why do you let her be so sullen?"

"Let her? You think I don't worry, every single night, that she doesn't want anything enough? You think I don't know what that means now?"

Hannah turned to go and closed the outer door loud enough for them to hear. She didn't care.

It wasn't true. She did want things. That is, she wanted to want things, even to love things, as much as Toby loved every living thing. Only she couldn't say what. It was too impossible now. Wanting anything seemed crazy.

And she did have a friend. Marie.

Marie passed notes to her in school all last year. The last note was that Marie could not go walking with her after school that day because she had to tend her baby brother, but the day after they didn't either, or ever did again. Now they were in different schools, and once when she saw Marie on a street outside the River Quarter, Marie pretended she didn't recognize her. Now Hannah never left the

River Quarter just so she wouldn't see her and have to repeat the moment. She did too care about some things.

At least Mother stood up for her. A little. Except when she said that about what made her this way. As if something wasn't right with her. What was missing?

She let out a long, deep sigh. She needed to blow her nose but had no handkerchief with her so she just sniffed and wiped with her hand.

The lime trees did have new leaves that were just unfurling. What for? she thought. She kicked a pebble on the sidewalk, and then saw two German officers coming the opposite way. For a moment the whole world stopped except the pebble that clattered on toward one tall black boot. Her heart turned to ice. A wetness moistened her underpants. Talking loudly, the men didn't seem to notice the pebble, or even her. They made no move to accommodate her on the narrow sidewalk. At the last second she stepped off the curb to let them pass, and twisted her ankle.

Things were happening. Bigger than preparations for Passover. Beyond the candle glow there were things. There were things. Nothing was the same. Hilde acted as if it was Great-grandmother Etty's time.

But Father didn't. He knew. Maybe that was why he was softer with her. She knew she exasperated him when she didn't do her lessons, but by Sabbath afternoon, he had forgotten. He took long walks with her, leaving Toby and his talkativeness at home, along the canals of the River Quarter, buying her a pickle from the wooden vat at the corner of Vrijheidslaan and Vechstraat, or to Koco's ice cream parlor. Or he'd take her to Sunday concerts at Middelaan Plantage, or to the Rijksmuseum. And, that one wonderful day, to the auction. Walking along, he would ask her about her schoolmates, her lessons, to try to get her to talk. She tried to tell him about Marie once, but she couldn't speak the words. He always seemed so tired afterward, letting his shoes fall to the floor in the bedroom, saying, she heard once, "Maybe a little progress, Edith."

Now it became clear to her what made her love the girl in the painting. It was her quietness. A painting, after all, can't speak. Yet she felt this girl, sitting inside a room but looking out, was probably quiet by nature, like she was. But that didn't mean that the girl didn't want anything, like Mother said about her. Her face told her she probably wanted something so deep so remote that she never dared breathe but was thinking about it there by the window. And not only wanted. She was capable of doing some great wild loving thing. Yes, oh yes.

Hannah lingered doing the errands, not wanting to go right home. In the grocers' shops there were queues all the way out to the streets even though less was displayed than last week. After four shops, she stepped out into the boulevard again.

Then she saw them.

Another family of yellow stars carrying suitcases was being herded down the middle of Scheldestraat.

To Westerbork. That place.

Why them? she wondered.

As they passed, for the flash of a second a little boy looked at her with frightened eyes. She dipped her head and walked on. A pain shot through her chest. Ignoring it seemed the same kind of betrayal as Marie's. She turned onto Rijnstraat and hurried home so fast she had a side ache.

She accidentally let the door slam when she came in. "No parsley, so I got celery, but no egg anywhere."

"No egg? Did you go to Ivansteen's?" Mother asked.

"And to three places on Scheldestraat."

"What'll we do? And those poor home-less refugees coming and not even a full Seder plate."

"It won't matter. In a matter of time, it won't matter at all."

"Hannah! Never say that. Don't let me ever hear you say that."

"What happened?" Hilde took the shank bone from her hands to examine it. "What happened out there on the street?"

Hannah slapped the celery onto the sink counter and turned to leave. "Nothing, Oma."

Hilde followed her. "What did you see out there?"

"Nothing. Just children jumping off porches holding open umbrellas. Playing parachutes. They do it whenever they hear planes. Haven't you noticed?"

She watched Hilde and Mother look at each other in puzzlement. No, of course they hadn't.

That evening with the house darkened, after her parents hid ten pieces of *hametz* around the house, Tobias did the ritual final search for *hametz* by candlelight. Using a feather, he brushed the crumbs into a wooden spoon with a seriousness Hannah couldn't remember from past years when it was more of a game.

"Where'd you get the feather, Toby?" Hannah asked.

"It's Leo's." He held it up and twirled it. "Look how it's purple on the edge. And wider on one side than the other. It came out in my hand as I was holding him. I didn't mean to."

No. He could never do the birds harm.

Father put the crumbs, the feather and the spoon into a paper bag to be burned the next morning. After Toby went to bed, when she thought he'd be asleep, she drew back the curtain that divided their bedroom and looked at him awhile. The boy in the street had the same curly hair as Toby. Bending to pull the blanket over him, she breathed the musty, innocent smell of rabbit and crayon and pigeon.

Before breakfast the whole family gathered on the porch, and Father struck a match and touched it to the edge of the bag.

"Two places, Sol," Hilde said. "To give it a good burning."

Hannah watched the black edge creep sideways across the bag, like the front line of an army, she thought, bringing a small wall of orange flame behind it until it touched the other black edge advancing to meet it. The Red Sea closing in instead of parting. Eventually the wooden spoon was a burnt bone of dying cinder on the bricks of the porch. Hannah stamped it out.

In the afternoon Father went walking with Toby, Hannah didn't know where, but she knew they'd end up at the Rotterdam Cafe in order to bring home for Seder dinner two of the refugee families who were living upstairs.

Except for the slow rhythmic crunch-crunch of Mother chopping nuts for the *charoseth,* and the coos of the pigeons echoing down the open air vent, the house was quiet. With everything nearly ready for the holiday at sundown, it seemed to Hannah that the rooms breathed expectation, as before a death, or a birth. She thought about that for a while, feeling it settle as she sat sideways in her father's chair at the dining table, fingering idly the scalloped edge of the white tablecloth.

Hilde wedged two candles in the silver candlesticks, arranged the Delftware basin and pitcher on the sideboard for washing the hands, dug a dust rag one last time into the sideboard carving and flicked it along the lower edge of the picture frame.

"You know what she's looking at out the window, don't you?" Hilde said.

"Her future husband."

Naturally she'd think that, Hannah said to herself.

"What do you think?" Mother asked from the kitchen doorway.

"Pigeons. Just pigeons," Hannah said.

"Pigeons? What do you mean by that?" Hilde said.

"I mean it doesn't matter what she's looking at. Or what she's doing, or not doing." She looked Hilde dead in the eye. "It only matters that she's thinking."

"Is that why you like her?" Mother asked in surprise.

"And because I know her."

Hannah stood up, went down the hallway and up the attic ladder. Leo was closest, dozing. She grabbed him first, and in a frenzied flapping of wings, twisted his neck until its tightness released under her fingers. Squawks of the others rang in her ears. She lunged to catch Henriette and skinned her knee. Two, three, four, each time that same soft popping underneath the feathers.

She came down the hallway staring straight ahead. Her hands trembled so much Mother noticed. Hannah looked down too and saw a wisp of feather underneath the nail of her forefinger, the smallest bit of gray breast down. She flicked it away. Mother and Hilde gaped at her, apparently unable to move. Hilde's lips pinched into a purple wound.

"Go wash your hands," Mother murmured.

Hannah turned, caught her foot on the hall runner, and lunged into the bathroom. She heard her mother's voice. "This is one time, in your son's home, you will say nothing, Hilde. Nothing." Hannah turned on the water. She didn't want to hear what would come next. She washed up to her elbows, and her skinned knee. After a while she slipped into her room and lay on her bed. When she heard through the air vent Mother sweeping the coop, she felt a trickle of moisture creep toward her temple. She waited for the chop-chop of the *charoseth*. Then she changed her dress and gave her hair a good brushing.

When Father and Toby came in, she couldn't look directly at them. The two German families were awkward, not knowing where to put themselves. A boy younger than Toby stood wordless and clinging to his father. Mother had Toby introduce each guest to Hilde, had him pass out the Haggadahs, had him bring the white *kittel* to his father to put on. She had him arrange on the Seder plate the celery, the shank bone, the *charoseth*, a withered root of horseradish and a small peeled potato carved narrower at one end to look like an egg, and then she asked him to watch on the porch for sunset in the western sky. All this, Hannah knew, so he wouldn't think to take the little German boy upstairs to show him the birds.

Mother rummaged in the sideboard and brought out the old Delftware candlesticks. "Here," she said to Hannah. "These were your great-grandmother Etty's, but tonight and forever, they'll be yours. Wash them and put them on the table."

And Hannah did.

"Sunset's coming," Toby announced from the porch. "The sky's all goldy."

Her mother struck a match and held it to an old candle stub until a flame rose, touched it to the two tapers in the silver candlesticks and handed it to Hannah. She did the same with hers. Watching her candlelight illuminate the girl in the painting, she knew why this night was different from all other nights. Real living had begun.

Adagia

Walking with his wife Digna along the narrow canal, Laurens van Luyken kept a discreet distance behind the young lovers, as if to give them privacy, but he watched their every move. Just beyond his neighbor's oxcart, he saw his daughter lean, unnecessarily, on the young man's arm.

The autumn air blew crisply and Digna drew close her cape. Laurens usually found wind invigorating, but this afternoon it made him feel as though a wall of gray sea were thundering toward him against which he had to brace himself. The breeze was crisp, the fallen leaves were crisp, everything was crisp. Johanna's voice was crisp earlier that day when she told him, "Papa, Fritz asked me to marry him, and I told him yes." Just like that. No prelude. No delicacy. Not even a nod to tradition. As if fathers needn't even be asked anymore to give up their daughters to someone else's love. Was this the way Amsterdammers did things? A herald of how life would be in the new century?

"We should give them a fine gift," Digna said, taking Laurens's arm just like Johanna had done with Fritz. "Something of ours she's always loved and will always keep."

"Does that mean you're agreeing to this?"

"He's a good fellow. And handsome." He caught her playful smile. "Erasmus says if you must be hanged let it be on a fair gallows."

"Gallows weren't intended for the young and innocent."

Up ahead their dog, Dirk, trotted right in Johanna's way so that she almost stumbled, and then Fritz said something that made her laugh. Laurens watched her press herself against this man and kiss him lightly on his ear. Dirk barked what Laurens knew was an admonition. Laurens found a perverse pleasure in noting that Dirk did not take too keenly to the attentions Johanna was paying to this odd-smelling interloper in leather shoes instead of good, solid *klompen,* clearly not a resident of Vreeland. He was amused when Dirk, trembling with suspicion, had growled something obviously insulting at Fritz when he arrived by coach at noon.

"Look at her, Laurens. Radiant."

Instead, he glanced sideways at his wife. The happiness had traveled: His daughter's wild, dewy bliss had freshened every pore in Digna's familiar face.

"What could we give them?" she asked, a pleasant urgency in her voice.

"A broom and a butter churn?"

"We could give them the *Digna Louise*."

"No. Fritz has an old smack boat. He told me he took it out last week to the Zuider Zee and nearly froze. No one in his right mind, outside fishermen, would go sailing there after September."

Their neighbors' skiffs were lined up stem to stern where the canal joined Loosdrechtse Plassen. Laurens remembered how as a young girl Johanna called them wishbone boats, for the graceful shape of their prows. He wondered if she told Fritz that just now as they passed the skiffs along the bank.

Johanna and Fritz turned at Ruyter's mustard mill to walk the lakeshore wagon road, and looked back for Laurens and Digna to follow. Something of their expectancy, the feeling that they were sailing forth into an adventure in an untried craft, awakened in Laurens a vaguely competitive warmth, and he slipped his arm around his wife's supple waist. "You cold?" he asked, half hoping that she was.

"I could give her my mother's opal ring, but that's not very much. And it should be something from both of us. For both of them."

To Laurens, everything about the couple ahead bore the conspicuous marks of euphoria. Too soon blooming, he thought, too soon coming in to seed. They had not suffered long winter evenings of soulful contemplation, but were careening ahead as if it were already tulip time.

So now she would go. She would leave Vreeland where she knew every pathway, every plank of every bridge, every family's horse and wagon, where he'd taught her to skate right here on Loosdrechtse Plassen, where he'd watched her play every summer under the willows at their canal edge, happily pouring buckets of canal water into a cracked and chipped Delftware tea set that had been his mother's. She would leave the town of her birth and ancestry, and go to Amsterdam, nearly half a day's carriage ride over the dike roads.

Laurens was amused that Dirk made such a show of his distrust of this wolf in sheep's clothing, this mountebank with the queer smell, by plunging his way between

Fritz and Johanna's legs, but Laurens did not gloat. Something moved him about the way they paid homage to each other with their eyes, Johanna shining with the intoxication of the unknown, and he wanted them to have a moment's peace. Only a thrown stick, well aimed along the narrow bank, would tear Dirk away from his self-appointed office of protecting Johanna. Laurens called to Dirk, threw the stick and missed the grassy bank. Dirk bounded into the lake to chase the splash, and Digna laughed, making it all worthwhile.

She squeezed his arm. "I know! The painting. *Girl With a Sewing Basket.*" Her bright expectant eyes and open-mouthed smile shot through him. "She's always loved it."

"No."

Dirk brought him the stick but he did not take it.

Digna turned to him, a look of bafflement on her sweet ivory face. He watched a breeze blow strands of her chestnut hair out from her chignon, waving like sea grass in a current. She pulled him along, laughing through her words. "What makes you so ungenerous? She's our only daughter."

"I'm sure we can think of something else."

"Why not the painting?"

"Because I gave it to you."

"But it would be a touch of our home in theirs."

"No, Digna."

"Why not?" She put her hand in his, urging his agreement.

"I wouldn't want to be without it."

"I never knew you were that attached to it. It isn't worth much, though I do like the way it mimics a Vermeer."

He grabbed on to that. "More like a de Hooch. The dealer said de Hooch painted floor tiles the same way."

She smiled a teasing reprimand, a smile recognizing the transparency of his diversion. He felt foolish and exposed. She knew him too well. No doubt she had some adage from Erasmus to warn about people who try lamely to change the subject. Digna rendered favorite epigrams from Erasmus's *Adagia* as embroidery samplers, sometimes keeping the Latin if she liked the way it sounded, like *"Tempus omnia revelat."* So earnest there by the fireside, over the years she stitched onto stretched cloth as if onto her heart Erasmus's religion of rational thought: Trying got the Greeks to Troy. An ill crow lays an ill egg. No one is injured save by himself.

"Why don't you give them an embroidery adage?"

Her smile turned to scornful laughter. "Why don't you want to give them the painting?"

He looked ahead toward the osier beds along the lakeshore. In the veiled atmosphere of a light fog blowing in, the osier heads bending and rustling seemed to him like ghosts beckoning.

"It . . . I bought it to commemorate a period in my life, and for that reason I can't let it go."

"I thought you bought it for me? Our anniversary. Remember?"

She pulled away and wrapped herself in her cape. A slight tremor passed through him.

"I did. I —" He was losing her now, but held onto the belief that they'd always trusted each other with truth. "It reminded me of someone I knew once."

Digna stopped.

"The way the girl is looking out the window," he said. "Waiting for someone. And her hand. Upturned, and so delicate. Inviting a kiss."

Digna turned. "Let's go back."

He looked ahead at his daughter and her man. "What about them?"

"They'll come."

When they headed back toward the house, Dirk ran before them, bounded back, and sprang forward again, knowing that at home he would be fed. Laurens felt a mild annoyance at his wild, glad movements.

Digna did not question him anymore, but slowed her pace, waiting. He looked out to the pewter-colored lake, agitated into peaked claws by gusts of wind, where he had courted danger many times, skating before the ice was ready.

"Her name was Tanneke. It was when I was working at the Haarlemmermeer pumping plant back in '74." He knew he should give this to her right then, to set the time, so long ago, years before he met Digna. "She lived in Zandvoort. I met her at The Strand, at the *poffertjes* stand. I elbowed my way ahead of her and bought a bagful, spun around and popped one in her mouth." He chuckled softly. "Powdered sugar stuck on her nose."

He longed to steal a glance at his wife, to see if she could imagine the scene to be as sweet and innocent as he remembered it.

The flow of memory as they walked kept him thinking out loud. "We used to go out walking. Along the dunes and in the heather. In the woods too. She loved Haarlemmer Hout, knew its paths as well as Johanna knows the lanes of Vreeland. I kissed her palm once, in those woods, under a fir tree where we'd gone for shelter from a rain."

"Were you in love with her?"

He'd said too much. He was sorry he'd mentioned anything.

"With her I was . . . I was like Fritz." He turned from her so she would not see on his face the happiness he had with Tanneke so long ago.

A gust of memory shivered him. "I was foolish. I didn't keep a rendezvous with her, so that I would appear independent, I suppose. To make her long for me, when it was really I who longed for her. When I went to see her some time later, she had left Zandvoort, and had told her parents not to tell me where she'd gone." A pang at his own stupidity, his passivity or lethargy, shot through him with surprising sharpness, which he hoped his voice had not revealed.

Staring ahead, he felt rather than saw Digna move away.

And now, stupid again, to hurt his wife. They went the rest of the way in silence, and he felt her trying to imagine her way into his past.

They passed the train of skiffs, and the wishbone shapes, inverted now, were to him only his neighbors' old rowboats. They passed their neighbor's vegetable garden, and he had to call Dirk back from trampling through the rows of purple cabbages sitting in enviable order. They passed the windmill of Vreeland, turning faithfully, grinding water out of the soil to keep their tiny island of the universe afloat forever. And they passed a place in their lives, he thought, where all these things — skiffs, gardens, dry land, love — could be maintained without conscious effort.

Dirk ran in wide circles around them, leaping, splashing through seeping puddles. When they got back to the house, his paws would be muddy and would have to be cleaned. Digna usually saw to that. Today he'd do it.

It was strange: When you reduced even a fledgling love affair to its essentials — I loved her, she maybe loved me, I was foolish, I suffered — it became vacuous and trite, meaningless to anyone else. In the end, it's only the moments that we have, the kiss on the palm, the joint wonder at the furrowed texture of a fir trunk or at the infinitude of grains of sand in a dune. Only the moments.

He wanted to remind Digna of some moment from their life together equally tender as the kiss in the woods, equally important. There'd been many, as when they skated far out on Loosdrechtse Plassen, so that voices of the other skaters were only rustlings of thrushes and they were swirling alone in a white, pure universe, and he had told her he had now known her half his life, twenty-two years, his breath heralding that miracle with clouds of fog, and he had kissed her there on the ice, twenty-two times, in gratitude. He longed to have her think of this, but how she walked, so erect and self-contained, staunched his throat.

As they approached the house he saw that before they'd left she had lit an oil lamp in the parlor for their return. The warm yellow light through the window beckoned them to a cozy house. She always thought of things like that. If he mentioned it now, or the skating memory, it would seem propitiatory.

In the house they stayed out of each other's way while knowing precisely each other's every move. The air between them felt charged.

He wanted her to come to him so he could stroke the smooth skin of her temple, a favorite part of her, right there by her hairline, hold her by the shoulders first, then draw her close to him, and say he was wholly hers and ever would be all his life.

But she busied herself with setting out the supper, a sure sign that she was not ready for affection, and so he did not do what he longed for most. Letting the moment go felt vaguely, uncomfortably familiar.

Then Johanna and Fritz came in talking of his work in Amsterdam, and he lost his chance.

"When you come to visit us, Papa, we'll go sailing," Johanna said, placating.

To them, life seemed exquisitely simple, clear as polished crystal. Oh, for them to know. Some day they'd know. It's only after years that one even notices the excruciating complexities.

With only enough words to keep up civility, Digna served the *hutspot*, and spent the supper hour flicking off crumbs from the tablecloth.

Laurens knew Johanna thought her mother's sudden change of mood had something to do with her, or Fritz. When Digna stepped into the kitchen to fetch the pudding, Laurens tried to assure Johanna, wordlessly, walking his fingers across the tablecloth to cover her hand like he used to do when she was a child, to make her laugh, or when he wanted to reach Digna if she had drifted from him.

He saw that Johanna's windburned cheeks gave off the rosy glow of a perfectly ripe peach. Notice. Pay attention. Notice this and never forget it, he wanted to say. He looked at Fritz who was only watching their hands, and the young man's confusion as to what was appropriate for him to think at this moment passed across his face. Laurens straightened himself in his chair and smiled the smile of one who is fully, intensely conscious, smiled broadly as if to say he would not surrender this fatherly right of his hand on hers. No, not just yet. Or ever.

Fingering his hat brim, Fritz left early and Johanna, breathless, turned from the closed door and said, "Aren't you happy for me, Papa?"

Studying the beauty of her cheek so that he would remember it in twenty years, he motioned her toward him.

"Isn't love absolutely the most stupendous thing? I mean, I know you and Mama love each other, but I wasn't prepared."

"Prepared?" The word alarmed him. He

knew Digna had not brought herself to discuss those womanly things.

"For the power."

Fearing a tremble in his voice, he did the only thing he could do: He kissed her lightly on the temple before she went upstairs.

Digna took up her embroidery. The cuckoo clock filled the silence. He watched Dirk scavenge what he could of dignity in the face of his mistress's distraction by settling at her feet and letting out a satisfied sigh. For a moment he envied Dirk's easy intimacy.

He didn't know what to say, what to offer her. He tried to conjure what she must have looked like when she was Tanneke's age. Hair the color of maple leaves in autumn was all he could imagine.

"What adage are you working on now?" he asked, to break the silence.

She held out the embroidery hoop for him to see. She'd just begun the stitching of a bridge across a narrow canal and a willow tree. The words underneath were done in cross-stitch. *"Ne malorum memineris,"* she said.

"What's that mean?"

Solemnly, in full control of the moment, she looked down at the hoop and took two more stitches, making him wait — the thread so long and slow, and that tiny "pook" sound as her needle punctured the stretched fabric. "Remember no wrongs."

It was something for which he had no reply.

He took his clay pipe outside and walked to the canal edge. The wind had died but he felt the dampness of fog and heard the sedge warblers settling in families for the night.

He remembered the satiny feel of Tanneke's hand in his, the weight of it, relaxed, turned upward, and how he felt so gallant when, stiff-backed and formal, new at love, he bent to kiss it, her little finger extended, curved just as in the painting, so inexpressibly delicate, thin as a wishbone, and simultaneously, the tiny, thrilling intake of her breath.

Like so many times at the pumping house, and much later when he looked at the painting, he indulged in imagining Tanneke and her braid of honey-colored hair, heavy in his hand when he unbraided it, and his life with her, what it might have been.

After that last walk in the woods of Haarlemmer Hout, he'd brought Tanneke home — her house had a stork's nest high on a pole, he remembered — and stayed outside until he saw her silhouette through the curtain carrying her candle to her upstairs bedroom, walking close to the window so he would see her, filmy and ethereal, how, slowly, deliberately, she lifted her dress over her head, and then her shift, and then, teasing him, she blew out the flame. He'd sat in the lane and thought of every part of that room he'd never seen, and now again he made up the details — the small porcelain stove in the corner with its slate hearth where she played as a child, her drawings pinned to the pale blue walls, the tall oval mirror where she appraised her womanliness, her hornbacked hairbrush, her washbowl and pitcher, Delftware probably, like his mother's, the bed with four turned mahogany posts, and the counterpane, peach and mint green perhaps, her grandmother's. And Tanneke naked underneath it. As he thought of these unseen things now, again, he felt that old warm coursing through his veins.

He couldn't honestly promise himself that that would never happen again.

His shame for it made him objective: Was it Tanneke herself that kept this memory alive all these years, or was it merely the euphoria of first love that he'd wished to preserve? The fact of the question occurring to him at all told him his answer. If Digna could only know, but more explanation would only keep her pain alive.

He'd wait a bit longer to give her time.

What had been so important that he let Tanneke wait and wait at the tram station? He couldn't imagine it to be work at the pumping house that had detained him. It was his need to seem important. But what he'd done that night instead, probably only something with his fellows, he could not remember. He paced along the canal edge to fill the vacancy of memory. Still he could not remember.

He had tried several times to find her, but he knew no friends of hers to ask. To lose someone in a country so small seemed ridiculous, although if he were really honest with himself, there had been a lassitude in his looking. For a while he was content with her phantom being, and then later, when something between curiosity and longing stirred him, he felt foolish to intrude on a life already half lived.

Now he knew, as he'd known a hundred nights when he looked at the smoothly painted upturned hand before he took the lamp upstairs, that there was nothing so

78

vital as paying attention, and perfecting the humble offices of love. And that he'd tried to do with Digna. Maybe in some small way that made less reprehensible his nightly complicity with the painting.

He breathed long and deeply, to expel the past and find his bearings in the present. With Johanna already old enough for love, all this imagining of the past seemed to be a squandering of the present. A flood of now washed over him, like water breaking through a dike, and he welcomed it. The shared pleasure of a good *hutspot* with sweet carrots and spring potatoes and big chunks of beef when coming in from a windy walk together. The winsome lilt of Digna humming in the garden. Her knowing, almost teasing look, not quite a smile, when she knew she had the upper hand about something, and his willing acquiescence. Her coaxing in the dark next to him — What was your favorite part of the day? — to which he'd always say, because he always thought it — now, touching you. He'd feel the lump of truth form in his throat, the swell of love in his loins. And afterward, the peace of her rhythmic breathing, steady as a Frisian clock, her simple, uncomposed lullaby. Those are things he would, in some final, stretched-out moment, relive. How love builds itself unconsciously, he thought, out of the momentous ordinary.

He finished his pipe, giving her time. Digna would think it through, he knew. It might take her a while, but she would eventually realize that it was imagination, not memory, that was her enemy, if she indeed had any enemy in this.

Digna blinked several times when he came in. She had on her good lavender dressing gown, which she seldom wore, and she was brushing her hair let down over her shoulders. "I took the advice of the painting," she said with a kind of urgent pride.

"What's that?"

"I stopped sewing." She smiled a tiny, wan smile. "I looked it up. *Memineris.* Erasmus says that after liberating Athens from the cruelties of the Thirty Tyrants, Thrasybulus made a decree prohibiting all mention of the past. They called the decree *amnestia.*"

Digna. Oh, Digna.

His eyes welled up and she appeared wavy as though through a glass, then only a blur of lavender, and he did not want even that transparency to be between them. He looked away so she would not see, at Dirk, curled and sighing at Digna's feet, so as not to look at the painting. Soon he'd have to travel half a day over rutted dike roads to see it. And he'd be watched. He imagined with horror the newly framed embroidery sampler declaring in careful stitches its decree of silence and amnesty, hanging within the discolored rectangle on the cream-colored wall. No, Digna wouldn't do that. She wouldn't put it there.

Involuntarily, he looked up to check if the painting was still hanging in its place.

After a time, he said, "If instead of looking out the window, the girl were looking in, at us, she would surely think we were enviable creatures."

That near-smile flicked across her face. "Look long enough," she said softly, "out or in, and you'll be glad you are who you are."

Whether she meant it as observation or exhortation, he would not ask, or imagine.

Hyacinth Blues

I have forgotten, I am ashamed to say, his face.

No, not Gerard's. His.

Now, it's not wise to be shocked. It makes one's face blotchy and you don't want that. I wouldn't tell just anybody, because there are parts, there are parts — but since you asked for counsel in such matters, I will tell you. The truth, that I did not love the husband my father chose for me, I had concealed more carefully than a breast.

That is to say, until I first saw *him*. He was playing in a small orchestra at that somber brick Mauritshuis — the new *Eroica* Symphony which we finally heard in The Hague two years after my sister heard it at the Beauvais — and he was wearing an elegant puce frock coat and red moire waistcoat with thin violet stripes. His breeches were not the same old black silk that Gerard wore day in and day out, but suede, fastened with bows and reaching farther down the leg. Surely he wasn't Dutch.

I have a thing or two to tell you about the Dutch, so I'm glad we have all afternoon. At that Mauritshuis concert, for example, Louis XVI fashions, ten years out of date, were still in evidence, too blatant not to humiliate them, but miraculously, they carried on without even seeming to notice. That woman loosely connected to the House of Orange, the former Baroness Agatha van Solms whom my husband thought charming, was still wearing side hoops. And her headdresses! She thought it clever to suggest her family's contributions to Dutch naval history by building a ship, a man-of-war I think it was, atop horizontal rows of cadogan curls — no one wore cadogan curls anymore — as if the vessel were bravely battling those ferocious blonde waves. On its stern she flew a tiny flag. Prudently, it was the flag of the Batavian Republic. A cheap way to advertise the role of the House of Orange in sea conquests, if you ask me. Add to this that she still followed that odious practice of tying a red velvet ribbon about her neck as an expression of sympathy for those caught by Madame Guillotine. Not a dram of taste.

Now, don't label me derisive or fault-finding. You didn't have to live there. Besides, there was one Dutch thing I loved. It was a small painting Gerard bought me of a young girl whose skin had the sheen of transparent peaches. She was looking out an open window with such a sweet, naive expression on her face, though at first I thought it a bit vacant. You see, the villagers are cut off from each other by water, always water. Such inbreeding that more than a few of the ladies are half-witted or decidedly curious in a bovine sort of way. Still, this child must have had parents who loved her, and that generated in me both tenderness and melancholy. Envy, I suppose it was, due to my own barrenness, awareness of which had begun to make Gerard irritable even earlier when we were in Luxembourg.

I placed the painting in the small drawing room, above a blue velvet chaise that intensified the blue in the girl's smock, which hung in graceful folds of that luscious deep blue of the early hyacinths when the blooms are just beginning to open, not the paler blue after they've waned. If I had a daughter, I would dress her in the colors of only the freshest hyacinths and tulips. And just as my sister

Charlotte does with her Cherise, I would parade her every spring at the Promenade de Longchamp. And she'd have pearls. So I made inquiries at the artists' guild to have a string of pearls painted in around the poor girl's naked neck.

Gerard said the painting was by a minor artist, some Johannes van der Meer. It didn't matter to me. The girl was lovely, and I claimed her with all my heart.

At first I thought the gift was a placating measure given so I would be content another year or two, until he could secure an appointment back in France. It was after Gerard had a solid month of conferences with the former Countess Maurits van Nassau at the Mauritshuis about some revenue waiver, or so he said, though I know different now. And that, my dear, is the real reason for such propitiatory gifts, so be wary.

Since the Countess Maurits was the concert hostess and a gracious lady in all respects, I called upon her the day after the concert in that mausoleum of a Mauritshuis where she lived, I can't imagine how. She received me in a room decorated with blue and white tiles on the fireplace and blue Delftware plates standing by the dozen upon shelves and sideboards. And on those plates, always bridges arching up in the air over rivers, and spineless weeping willow trees. Who would want that symbol of melancholia staring at you? I had enough of the real thing, thank you. Poor woman, she couldn't get a decent Ishfahan, or even a Hamadan. Just a Flemish, and chintz everywhere, and two Frisian cuckoo clocks quacking every few minutes — enough to give you the vapors.

Though denuded of her title by The Emperor, she still displayed her wealth upon her ample bosom, somewhat like deflated meringues sad to say, the left one marked by a small mole, but I couldn't be sure; it may have been painted on. She informed me that the violinist was Monsieur le C—, fresh from Paris, and that he was to appear in a matter of weeks as guest performer playing Mozart's Symphony no. 40 in G Minor with the state orchestra, formerly the Royal Orchestra, at the Binnenhof.

"Oh, I do so love minor keys," I whispered. "His bowing technique, of which I am obviously not entitled to speak, certainly had me enraptured." I gave her a beseeching look on the final word.

With the intuition of the subtlest of women, surely a vestige of her lost title, she smiled understandingly. "He is staying for the summer at the Oude Doelen."

That was all I needed.

The Hague was small, only the size of three or four of the grand squares of Paris and their neighborhoods. I knew the Oude Doelen. Gerard and I had stayed there while our home for the duration of his commission was being prepared for us. But first, I had to secure an invitation to the Binnenhof concert. And, second, I had to have a new gown.

There was not a day to waste. Not a dressmaker on van Diemensstraat knew the styles in Paris. Nor did I, exiled as it were, first to Luxembourg and then to The Hague, while Josephine's salons exploded with new styles. And the tiny Dutch shops were no help. As empty as cells, those shops. Why they couldn't smuggle bolts of silk as well as casks of saltpeter is owed entirely to the dullness of the Dutch.

And another thing: You should thank the blessed Virgin, my dear, that God has spared you the uncharitable corset makers in The Hague. I tell you they have not an ounce of mercy — the resentment of the conquered toward his conqueror — no tender little words of understanding when they fit you, unlike Madame Adèle, my own corsetière, who says, I can hear her now, "It's only a question of rearranging the skin, madame." You really ought to try her. She does wonders in lifting the fallen. Rue St. Honoré just off the Place Vêndome.

Nevertheless I set out to clothe myself anew, not just top to toe but air to skin, just in case. My sister Charlotte had written to me that women were beginning to wear pantalets, and then she described them. Even if they were made of sheer lawn, oh, the discomfort of having rasping cloth there. Discreetly, I asked at a few shops. Not having heard of such a thing, they looked at me askance, so I had to content myself without, even though that distressed me somewhat. Surely Monsieur le C— knew more of what was being worn in Paris than I did, and I hated to be found wanting.

Now where did I leave off? Oh, yes. The Binnenhof. A plain palace from the outside that stretched along the south bank of the Vijver. It redeemed itself, though, once one entered the Trêves Zaal, where the concert would take place, a splendid white and gold reception hall imitating Louis XIV style, quite like the Galerie Dorée of the Hotel de Toulouse. The painted ceiling was dreamlike with clouds and cherubs, and so I was prepared to think the violinists, Monsieur le C— especially, were descending to us from Heaven.

I worked my way toward the first few rows of seats and Gerard followed. The musicians were already seated, and there he was, first violinist, concentrating on tuning the orchestra. His white lace jabot frothed under his dear chin like a whipped dessert. The first movement, *molte allegro*, was a sprightly melody — tra-la-la, tra-la-la, tra-la-la-*lá* it went, and his hands flitting about cast a spell on me. Hardly able to breathe in the sudden heat, I batted the air with my fan. By the happiest of chances, the gesture seemed to attract Monsieur le C—'s eye.

He noticed me. Yes, I was sure of it.

During the long *andante* his eyelids drooped provocatively over his instrument, and his bowing arm caressed the strings as if they were the heartstrings of his beloved. He played the *andante* with such tenderness I nearly fainted. He must have been a child prodigy, some doting mother's darling. By the fourth movement I was dizzy to the point of rapture. You know the feeling or you wouldn't have asked me.

As for Gerard during all of this, I

couldn't say. He busied himself more and more with his columns of figures, with dispatches, and especially with the disenfranchised Dutch nobility. He bought a painting by a Dutch artist and began to smoke a long porcelain pipe. My husband, I am sorry to say, was becoming Dutch.

I can't be sure but his defection may have started a year earlier. I remember it was late spring because the hyacinth on my dressing table had reached that stage of sadder, paler blue when its fragrance was most poignant because it was offering up the last of its zest. I had not yet executed my morning glories, that is to say, my morning rites at the dressing table. I had no plaster or powder on yet, and had not put on my ringlets. I was plucking when Gerard said something to me that I didn't hear; truth to say, though I rue it now, I ignored him because I cannot think, much less actually speak, when I am doing my face.

"Claudine!" he said, so loud it startled me and I dropped my tweezers.

The notion of lovers living together is altogether too demanding. One can be caught so unready. When you get to be my age, you'll understand.

In the mirror I saw him looking at me,

sitting on the edge of the bed without his breeches and without his stockings too, so his thin hairy legs dangled off the end of the bed like a spider.

I turned to him and said sweetly, "What is it, *mon cher?*" Always be sweet, no matter what. You never know what's on their minds.

He didn't say what he'd intended to, the words must have flown away like moths, but he had the look of a man to whom something had happened. His eyes were distressed, as though he saw for the first time that our possibilities had been checked, that the son he had imagined would never be. I think it suddenly occurred to him that we had stopped trying to have a child. At that moment I suspected that whatever hold I had on him was slipping. Afterward, a heaviness sat on my heart.

I was brought up to believe that when one marries according to family wishes, with time and patience, love will come, so I had made an effort at love even though I didn't quite know what I was striving for. Oh, there had been occasions of passion, but was that love? I had a sentimental notion, to answer your question, that love meant one would risk all, sacrifice all, overlook and endure all in order to be one with the beloved. I used to hold dear the doctrine — borrowed from my aunt in Provence — that if one acts with sufficient passion in all things, then that passion will correct whatever might be unfortunate in one's circumstances. But after that look — Gerard's eyes so full of disappointment, as if the world had changed and he recognized it finally for what it was, and would never call it beautiful again — after that look, I was no longer certain of my aunt's doctrine.

I tried to make the best of things, for he was good enough to me after a fashion — gave me a painting of a girl, my wish, not a boy, his, you see — though he was good enough to others too. It was no secret that he'd been well occupied during his period as *ministre d'impôt,* collecting for The Emperor 100 million guilders a year, but exacting less tangible taxes from some privately chosen devalued Dutch nobility, chiefly amongst them that former Baroness of the House of Orange flying the flag on a curl. I resolved to ignore that and not to think, and for the next year I occupied myself with pleasant things, like organizing excursions to the tulip fields of Haarlem in the spring, and in summer braving the wicked sea wind at Schveningen to shiver in those funny wicker tub chairs on the strand, and in the winter having skating parties at the Huis ten Bosch. On the ice once, Gerard, nearly falling, let out a little whoop of terror and laughed at himself and reached impulsively for my hand, and I was overwhelmed with tenderness for him, though I wouldn't call it love. He would have reached for any hand to right himself.

And now, thanks to the Countess of the Mauritshuis, I knew that Monsieur le C— could, with his swirling variations on a theme, sweep away the despair of my restlessness.

I sent a message to the Oude Doelen, inviting him and three others of his choosing, a string quartet, to give a chamber evening in our home, "an ample white stone mansion on the Vyerburg," I wrote, so he'd know he would get an audience of substance. He replied cordially, and with that encouragement I called upon him the next day for the purpose of making arrangements. When he received me, the immaculate whiteness of his neck linen sent me into a swoon, but luckily, with my smelling salts and his firm hand at my back, I was able to recover. I invited, breathlessly. That is to say I determined not to breathe again until he assented. He tipped his head in consideration, arched a perfectly plucked eyebrow, straightened the lace at his cuff, gave a slow, practiced smile, and suggested that we take a carriage ride in the Bosch, the great wood outside the city.

We did so, with the curtains down. So steamy it was in that close, rumbling box — it was July — that I couldn't bear it. My fichu was stuck to the damp back of my neck and in the front to my allurement mounds as well. I had no choice but to remove it. In the dim light I discovered as I looked down and sideways — coquettish still, I hoped — that on his waistcoat an entire landscape was worked in petit point. When I took the liberty to run my hand across the stitching, he covered my hand with his, pressing it to him, a sure sign that he had agreed to assemble a quartet. I could breathe!

"Haydn is *de rigueur*," he said, "but might I suggest as well the Mozart Quartet in C Major? It's called 'The Dissonant.' Does that frighten you?"

"On the contrary, it sounds thrilling."

"It begins with a pulsing bass note, like the heartbeat of a man expectant of fulfillment, and then swells to fullness as the higher voices join."

"Does it . . . does it reach *crescendo?*"

"With sublime consummation."

"Then we shall have it."

The next week he sent word by messenger that he had secured the other members of the quartet, and a few days later I called upon him again to discuss the guest list and finalize the evening's musical program, which we did while taking a walk around the feather-flecked Vijver to view the swans.

"It's always politic," I said, "to have some Patriots in attendance, so I have invited the families of Leopold van Limbourg Stirum, Gijsbert Karel van Hogendorp, and Adam van der Duyn.

"Did you know that swans mate for life?" he asked. "What do you think about that?"

"Foolish. See how tiny their heads are?"

The evening of the chamber concert, I wore silk faille, the color of a hyacinth, like the girl's smock in the painting, not too showy, but certainly noticeable. In a last-minute inspiration, I had sent our houseman all over the city looking for hyacinths to dress the grand salon. The scent would be intoxicating. While waiting for his return, I paced the rooms, moist under my arms and breasts. I bathed again, pouring cool water over my neck to calm me, and listened to the sounds of the house — Gerard humming in his dressing gown, off-key but happily; staccato steps on the marble floor, chairs being arranged in the salon, hushed voices urging, "No, no, Madame said you're to put it *there*," and "Madame said we must not light the oil lamps in the drawing room, and the *petite salle* must be kept dim." It would be ever so lovely, everywhere one looked, those plucky columns of sweetness in all shades of blue standing stiffly up like, like . . . yes, well, this would be a night, I told myself, when ladies sheathed in spangled moonlight would feed on blossoms drenched with honey.

When the houseman finally did return, I saw at once that it was too late in the summer. "No hyacinths, madame. Dreadful sorry. I went to every flower shop I know." He held forward one bedraggled bloom, embarrassingly past its prime. To avoid comparison, I thought it wise not to exhibit it.

The grand salon glowed golden with fresh tapers in the sconces. Pastel guests skimmed across black and white floor tiles polished so that the whole surface seemed coated with glass. Across tinkling laughter,

Gerard bent gallantly to kiss the hand of that Orange woman, Agatha of the preposterous headdresses, who was, no doubt, sewn into her gown. I searched the depths of my heart for the graciousness to greet that woman kindly, but a feather bird nested in organdy on her cabriolet bonnet fell forward at each nod of her head so that it appeared to be pecking for food. I didn't trust myself.

Suddenly there he was!

He wore a sleek tailcoat with a pattern of sea-green scales. When he turned to greet Gerard, I could see the tails tapered into points like the tail of a cod. From the back, he looked, *mon Dieu!* he looked like — a fish, a veritable fish! I couldn't breathe. I couldn't think. He began to make his way toward me when he was intercepted by the Countess Maurits, and then others, and I had to content myself by greeting him without a private word.

During the Haydn I adopted the attitude I imagined him to cherish — a lofty, ethereal dreaminess. I leaned forward to show I was intensely interested, although it shot a pain through my lower back, and the vertical bones in my corset dug into my stomach — which would not have happened had we been in Paris where we belonged.

I noticed Gerard looking around the room distractedly instead of paying full attention to the notes. How could anyone not keep his eyes fastened on the musicians?

I concentrated on Monsieur le C—'s mouth, how he puckered it in a precious little pout when he had to play something *allegro*. His hands, how deft and light, like birds. And his plucking! My heartstrings vibrated. To create such heavenly sounds, such moods, to have the power so to lift the spirit — was it any surprise that he stirred my passion? Heartwrenchingly, I wondered, as you are, if that could be the budding of love. I wasn't quite sure how to identify it. Was it something that made one all aflutter, or gave one an inner pool of great calm? That sounded too aged. Like a cheese. I preferred the flutter of birds, and my mind gamboled under their spell for all of the Mozart.

After an appropriate time mingling with the guests, I approached him, said that he played like an angel, and let him kiss my hand. It was not difficult thereafter to lure him into the drawing room. I only had to say I had a small Dutch masterpiece to show him. "A painting of a young girl, a virgin," I taunted, though now I'm ashamed I used her so. Passing through the *petite salle,* I turned down the wick in the oil lamp, then took his hand and led him to the darkened drawing room and quickly closed the door behind us. We could see nothing.

I counted the six steps to the divan and we sank into sinful luxury with a sigh. He kissed. I kissed, and I discovered, with the very tip of my tongue, a callous under his left jawbone. With a start I realized that must be where he squeezed the violin with his jowl, an occupational malady I could forgive for the grace of his bowing arm.

And I did forgive, for his hands played me like a beloved instrument. He danced his fingers across my throat *pianissimo* and executed a *glissando* down my spine. His prelude, an *arpeggio* trilling through my entire being. His plucking, all that I had hoped for.

Desperately he was rustling through dress, chemise, petticoat, crinoline and shift, and I thought with gratitude how impractical pantalets would have been. Breathing. There was deafening breathing and such rustling. Was he suffocating under there? So as not to be indelicate, I'll just say that his strings were swelling into a *vibrato.* He uttered a soft cry, in *tremolo,* until he sang one thin note, *falsetto*.

Was it my imagination or did I hear devilish stifled laughter? Decidedly feminine. We were not alone! Moreover, we might have been seen coming in the door at that moment of illumination. Lighting a lamp would tell me who it was, that is to say, who must be presented with a lavish gift, and quickly too, so that she would remain silent. Under my billowing gown Monsieur le C— stirred, and seemed about to begin the second movement, but I was so distracted by that presence, the rustling of fabric — taffeta it was — that all pleasure I had imagined for weeks flitted as quickly as a grace note. I tried to think who had been wearing taffeta this late into summer. I pushed myself away from him, felt for the table, struck a match and in the first flicker of lamplight saw, on the chaise beneath the chaste eye of the girl in the painting, with his breeches lowered like a plucked goose, Gerard.

And with him, not that Agatha creature of the bird's nest headgear, but the Countess Maurits, both of them staring at both of us.

I was caught, yes, but released too, in the same instant. Heaven's blessing! This would send me back to Paris!

I had only one alternative. Quickly, though without one shoe, I swept through the *petite salle* to the grand salon and marshaled the Baroness of Orange to witness his disarray. Like it or not, Agatha van Solms was going to countenance the infidelity of her lover.

It was, in all respects, an eventful night. I wouldn't give a thousand placid summer days in exchange for it. When I settled under the bedclothes toward dawn, Gerard was still raging.

"How dare you compromise my position here! You realize, don't you, that it will be all over The Hague tomorrow?"

Those were, I believe, the last words I heard that night as I turned on my side, raised the bedclothes over my ear, and remembered with a chuckle how, on my way back through the *petite salle* with Agatha in tow like a Dutch barge, I had collided with Monsieur le C— slinking his way out. I fell asleep thinking: What a shame we didn't have hyacinths.

Bitterness was out of the question. That I did not charge him with his various infidelities; that I did not attack that matron of the Mauritshuis who, God give her mercy, first introduced me to the pleasures of Dutch musical salons; that I was, in fact, indifferent to my husband's indiscretions testified, to me foremost, that our love was of a tepid paleness. The Hague was, every Dutchman declared pridefully, the very capital of reason above passion. Therefore, what I had been taught to fear, now I embraced. Betrayal — his or mine, it didn't matter — freed me. Best to leave quickly than become a byword of reproach mentioned behind linen fans out of range of daughters' ears. A season of contrition among the plumbago at my aunt's summer house in Provence, and then I would be back in Paris, at Charlotte's, where there would be theater and opera to keep me from thinking. Ah, that sublime, escaping sigh one sighs when one unlaces one's corset, that exquisite freedom could be mine with only a coach ride back to Paris.

But how to pay for it? Impossible to wait for my father to send me money. That would take a fortnight. And there would be questions. It would be indecent to stay here a night longer than necessary. I had to think. This time, I really truly had to think. What could I do? What did I have?

With a stab of pain, it came to me — the painting.

Trying not to look, I wrapped it in muslin the next morning and called for the carriage. The papers, which Gerard kept in his strongbox, I would have to do without. I started at van Hoep's, but encountered only niggling there. Standing up as if to go, the muslin in my hand, I couldn't keep my eyes from the girl in the painting. What I saw before as vacancy on her face seemed now an irretrievable innocence and deep calm that caused me a pang. It wasn't just a feature of her youth, but of something finer — an artless nature. I could see it in her eyes. This girl, when she became a woman, *would* risk all, sacrifice all, overlook and endure all in order to be one with her beloved.

"This is more than a pretty curio, my good man," I said. "You are looking into the guileless soul of maidenhood."

There was, I realized then, something indecent about behaving as we had in front of her. The shock to her sensibilities would leave indelible marks.

"Are you sure it's a Vermeer?" the dealer asked.

"Positive. There are papers, but at the moment they are inaccessible to me."

"And the papers indicate — ?"

"That it was painted by Jan van der Meer of Delft, and auctioned in Amsterdam about a hundred years ago. I can't remember when or where." I flipped my handkerchief to indicate that such details were of no consequence.

"There's no signature. If there was any chance those papers said a van Mieris, I'd give you two hundred guilders, but for only a Vermeer, phugh."

I wrapped the painting again and left without a word more, took it to a second dealer and said it was a van Mieris.

"Are you sure it's not a Vermeer?"

"I'm certain."

Again he asked for documents, but without papers testifying it as a van Mieris, he offered me only twenty-four guilders. Barely enough for a hired coach and inns to Paris. I accepted, and cried all the way home in the carriage.

Grâce à Dieu, Gerard was at the ministry. I had time for only a quick note to Charlotte: "I am escaping to France. Prepare Father. Let's spend the rest of the summer in Provence."

When my trunks were loaded and I was helped into the coach, what I felt was not a weeping, but a longing to weep that I mastered all too easily. Gerard would survive, and thrive. If there was anything to weep for, it wasn't Gerard, or Monsieur le C—, or even me. It was the painting, for now it would go forth through the years without its certification, an illegitimate child, and all illegitimacy, whether of paintings or of children or of love, ought to be a source of truer tears than any I could muster at parting.

Love as I knew it was foolish anyway, all that business about blood boiling and hearts palpitating, all that noticing of eyeballs. Think realistically, my dear. Who wants to peer into a quivering nostril anyway? If, indeed, that was love, it wasn't enough. I came to see that knowing what love isn't might be just as valuable, though infinitely less satisfying, as knowing what it is. Looking out the coach window at men and women bending over flat potato fields, I determined I would be just as content as my lost girl gazing out her own sunlit window. A great deal can be said for just sitting and thinking. Life is not, nor has been, a *fantaisie,* but one can still amuse oneself, no? And as for Monsieur le C—, though his face eludes me, I still say an *ave* for him every Passion Sunday at the Church of the Madeleine, as a way of thanking him from the strings of my heart for my resurrection.

Morningshine

Saskia opened the back shutters and looked out the upstairs south window early the second morning after the flood. Their farmhouse was an island apart from the world. Vapors of varying gray made the neighboring four farmhouses indistinct, yet there was a shine on the water like the polished pewter of her mother's kitchen back home. Let the waters under the heavens be gathered together unto one place, and let the dry land appear, and it was so, she thought. But it wasn't so. And the cow would have to stay upstairs with them until it was so, however long that was, stay upstairs messing the floor and taking up half the room.

She leaned on the sill and peered across the water to the bare elm tree, so small and new it was only a few twigs above the water, to see if their chickens were in it. Maybe Stijn would find them today. She felt the loss of Pookje the most. She was the beauty, with those chestnut feathers soft as baby's hair under her throat. And how she always rose so dainty-like and proud to show the perfect egg she produced. Then Saskia felt ashamed. Others had lost more than a few hens.

She and Stijn had hardly lost anything. The day of the flood she'd made dozens of trips upstairs carrying furniture and food, while the cow's big brown eyes followed her each trip. She tried to make a game of it for the children, and even went down into the cold water to feel around and rescue a few more things after the flood came. By the end of the day her legs ached and her arms hung limp as rags. She had thought Stijn would be pleased that she had gotten so much upstairs, but when he came in through the window after working on the Damsterdiep Dike for two days straight, he took one look at the clutter, and her grandmother's spinning wheel atop hurriedly stacked peat blocks, and said, "Do we need all this?"

She'd forgiven him. He was exhausted and preoccupied.

Now, out the south window, she noticed something dark floating on the water a long way away, turning as if by its own will, first one way and then another.

"Stijn," she said. "Would you look at that, now?" She felt his warm hand on her shoulder as he looked out with her. She had of late — and she knew this annoyed him — milked every chance touch or meaningless encounter for its loving possibility, and so she paused in speaking, so he wouldn't take his hand away. "Isn't that Boswijk's mare floating there?"

She turned to see him squint, to see those dear, new lines fan out from his eyes.

"It is, surely." He reached for his reefer and climbed out the north window on the other side of the house where he'd tied up his skiff.

Marta and Piet slipped out of bed and clamored over the linen chest to the sill beside their mother. "See," Marta said in her superior, know-everything voice of four years, "horses can too swim."

"That horse isn't swimming. That horse is just tall enough to poke his head up," Piet said.

Saskia gave them both a piece of cheese. There was no more bread. She'd have to learn how to bake in the little peat brazier.

"Saskia!" Stijn's voice rattled an alarm through her.

She squeezed between the cow and a sack of grain to the opposite window. From the rowboat, Stijn handed up to her something flat wrapped in a blanket. She leaned far out the window. It wasn't heavy but it slipped from her grasp beneath the blanket and fell into the muddy water. Stijn lunged for it, rocking the boat, grabbed it, disentangled the blanket and handed up again a painting. She brought it safely over the sill and stared at a beautiful girl looking out a window.

"What is it, Mama?" Marta said.

"My God!" she heard Stijn say. "Saskia!"

She leaned far over the sill and he stood up in the boat and handed her, more carefully, a baby in a basket, then seized the oars.

"A baby! Someone put a baby in our boat," Saskia said.

"A baby. A baby!" Piet echoed. He was five, just at that age where he mimicked everything he heard, and where everything in the world made him laugh.

She unwrapped the blanket, and the baby became smaller and smaller. It was so young, its face was still rose-colored and puckered. When she got to the sad-colored shawl, dull blue woven with gray-green, her hands shook and she stopped, for she knew the shawl had to be the mother's.

"Who, Mama?" Marta asked.

"I don't know. Poor thing, so cold."

"St. Nicholas!" Piet said. "St. Nicholas

put it there." Both children rolled on the floor in laughter.

She lighted a peat block in the brazier to heat water, and prepared to feed and wash the baby. She began to unwrap the shawl and found a wilted cabbage leaf. She smiled.

"What's that for?" Marta said, so close beside her she could hardly move.

"Oh, it's just an old superstition. Good luck for the baby."

"Can we keep it? Can we keep it, Mama?"

"The cabbage leaf?" Piet said.

Marta gave him a little shove. "Can we keep the baby?"

With trembling hands, Saskia lifted from a fold in the shawl a paper, some sort of art document. On the back, printed in big letters, were the words, "Sell the painting. Feed the child."

"Father in Heaven!" she murmured. The black letters swam like eels before her eyes. To think a mother could write that. She lifted away a wet rag. A boy. A little Moses boy with blue eyes and a few wisps of blond hair. A boy, if she could keep him alive. She put a pot of milk on a grate over the burning peat. She searched in the linen chest for diaper cloths and cleaned and fed

110

him by the time Stijn came back.

"It was Boswijk's mare," he said. "Dumbest horse I've ever seen. I got it roped and rowed it to his barn, but the damned thing wouldn't go up the ramp, so Boswijk's boy and I had to hoist him from the block and tackle in a sling. Now I missed the punt to the sea dike and will have to row."

"We've been given a charge, Stijn."

"That baby?" He looked down at him, not without kindness, but briefly.

"It's a boy." She knew that would make him more acceptable.

"Mighty skinny. Probably won't live more'n a week."

She showed him the paper. "The only name it gives is who made the painting." He turned it over. There followed a silence so long she wondered if they would ever speak again. "A charge from Heaven," she whispered.

"Aye, and the means to carry it out too. Take it to Groningen next market day."

"The baby?" She shot him an apprehensive look, for there was an orphanage there.

"The painting." Stijn wrapped up a hunk of cheese and a slab of salt pork and climbed out the window into his boat.

The boy was a perfect baby. The shape of his cheeks and the point of his chin seemed to her to form an open tulip. All day she sat feeding him drip by drip, her finger in his mouth, and the milk pouring down her finger. She kissed the bottoms of his feet and kept him warm and couldn't keep from touching him. Every so often he flung his arms open wide, as if to embrace her and the children and the cow and the whole world. They'd have to make inquiries, but in the meantime, God had charged her to keep this boy alive.

Every few hours Marta asked, "What are we going to do, Mama?" And Piet echoed, "What are we going to do?" Most times, she just smiled at them without an answer.

Stijn came home discouraged. Nothing would drain until they repaired the sea dikes. Then the drainage mills could begin working, and when the water got to the crown of the Damsterdiep Dike, then they'd go to work on that. "They're conscripting from as far inland as Woldijk. Those men are given lodgings in Delfzijl, but from here we'll have to punt every day."

She stretched up to kiss him on the cheek.

"Don't touch me. I'm filthy."

She had seen that, but it didn't matter. She drew back.

"It'll be a miracle if we'll get a spring planting," he said.

"We will. I know we will." She put her hand on his arm and felt the muscle tighten. He had a tendency to see the worst, and it was her job to keep him hopeful. "The baby took milk five times today."

He looked at the basket where she'd laid him. "What kind of mother would leave a baby in a flood?" He took off his outer clothes and sat on the edge of the high cabinet bed built into the wall. Piet, in the children's bed underneath, tugged at his pantleg. Stijn moved his leg out of reach.

"One who had no choice."

"St. Nicholas left it," Piet said, and then Saskia remembered. A stranger in a skiff who asked for milk.

"Ssh, Piet. Go to sleep." She poured a basin of dirty dishwater out the window. "He's a good baby." Just then, when Stijn was looking at him, the baby flung his arms wide. "See? He likes you."

Over the next days Stijn was gone at first light and came home after dark, *doedmoe*, as her own father used to say, dead tired.

113

All he had energy for was to eat and say a few sentences about the work. She was afraid to bring up the question of naming the baby, for that would seem to make him theirs. Once, when changing him, she called him Jantje, little Jan, after the name on the paper, and Piet and Marta took it up in the daytimes, but at night they didn't.

The house was to Saskia a happy isle in the midst of flood. She did everything in the cramped space between sacks of groats and their downstairs chests and table, and of course, Katrina, the milk cow. Each day, Saskia put down fresh straw and laid the dung cakes on the sills and roof to dry. They'd use them later to reconstitute the soil. Then she and Piet, who suffered the confinement more than Marta, rowed across to the barn to stack the dried dung and replenish their supply of grain, potatoes and pickled meat, and to get hay for Katrina. Because they needed milk, the cow had to stay, but Stijn led their plow horse down from the loft on the earthen ramp into the floodwaters and, from the rowboat, guided him, swimming, to the canal where all the villagers' horses were hoisted on a barge to dry pasture inland. With a cast iron oven set on the brazier, she could make round buns instead of the loaves she normally made in the big oven downstairs. She'd lugged the churn upstairs so she could make butter. They would survive. And so would Jantje. He kicked and wiggled and sometimes spit up, but his little voice grew stronger each day. His eyes looked up at her with gratitude, she imagined, that made her heart burst. In the evenings, her happiness, her reports of the events of the day, seemed only to aggravate Stijn.

This wasn't going to be a devastating flood like in the Bible. And it wasn't like the St. Elizabeth flood of three hundred years ago that swept away whole villages. She remembered a grim painting belonging to her grandmother that hung above the virginal at home. *Groot Hollandse Waard* it was called, and it pictured a once populous village that had become a permanent lake. Spires of drowned churches protruded amidst reed beds and nests of wading birds. Underneath, there was a sober warning: "The Lord God brought humankind up from the vasty deep and made him wax mighty. Likewise, He hath power to consign the evil ones to the consuming deluge." As a child, she'd been fascinated by the painting, but later, when she learned to read, the saying appalled her. She didn't like to think of a God of wrath.

When a flood brings a baby *and* a thing of beauty, it was not the Apocalypse, nor even a winnowing of souls. It was only water lapping four feet deep.

One rare warm day, she put all three children into the boat, lowering the baby in his basket on a sling from the gable beam pulley, just so they could get outside. She breathed deeply and rowed very slowly to enjoy it longer. The motion of the water put Jantje to sleep. She rowed to the four other houses in the hamlet and asked at the windows if they had seen the stranger in a skiff come through again. Stranger? There's nothing but strangers coming through all the time now with so many men repairing the dikes, they said. She told them of the baby, and showed his sleeping, pink face. "It'll be a long sight before he'll dig a garden for ye," one woman said. Boswijk's wife, Alda, gave her some molasses. Back home, she dripped some into his mouth from a spoon every once in a while. Marta sat next to him by the hour, waving a cloth above his face to see if his eyes would follow it, and at the first sign that they did, Saskia celebrated by putting molasses in the dough to make sweet cakes for the children.

As for the painting, she had hung it on a clothes peg to get it out of the way. In the evenings she hung clothes in front of it, so Stijn might not be reminded, but in the day she uncovered it. Sometimes she propped it in the pale slant of light coming in the south window. One morning clear and bright after a rain when they'd collected fresh water in the small roof cistern and buckets roped to the eaves, she washed off the painting, and oh, how it shone, more brilliant even than before. The russet of the girl's skirt glistened like maple leaves in autumn sun. Pouring in the window, creamy yellow light the color of the inner petals of jonquils illuminated the young girl's face and reflected points of light on her shiny fingernails. *Morningshine,* she called it, for her grandmother had told her that paintings had names.

"You'll be just like her someday," she told Marta as she braided her hair. She made up stories of the young woman in Groningen or Amsterdam or Utrecht, how she became famous for her sewing and people from all around would come to have a garment made by her.

If only she would be allowed to keep the painting too. She didn't have many beautiful things, didn't even have a china cupboard, only a floor chest covered with her grandmother's blue linen table scarf. Only one chair with a cushion. Only four painted plates tilted on the shelf, and a pewter measure. Nothing like the whitewashed kitchen stacked with Delftware in the big farmhouse where she grew up just outside of Westerbork, and Mother's long mahogany dining table and Grandmother's virginal in the front room and paintings on the walls and curtains of pale blue flax.

The girl in the painting had a blue smock. How glorious to drape oneself in blue — the blue of the sky, of Heaven, of the pretty little lake at Westerbork with the tiny blue brooklime that grew along the banks, the blue of hyacinths and Delftware and all fine things. To live and move and have her being in a flow of blue. She held Jantje up to the painting. "See, Jantje, how beautiful she is. Maybe this is your mother. See how young she looks? A fine lady in a fine home." If that was so, Jantje had to know that his mother wore blue. The shawl was not blue enough. Besides, it was old and torn. He needed the painting.

It wasn't only Jantje who needed it. The Oriental tapestry on the table, the map on the wall, the engraved brass latch on the window — since Saskia couldn't have these things in reality, then she wanted them all the more in the painting. For the moments when she was filled with the joy of Jantje blowing bubbles out his tiny mouth, or when Piet made her laugh at his antics, or when Marta ate her bread with her little finger extended like a lady at tea, the grip of wanting left her and she was at peace. But that wasn't constant.

"This boy came from a fine family," she told Stijn one night. He looked at her, apparently too tired to ask with words how she knew. With shoulders slumped, he waited for her explanation. "Just look at that lace on the edge of the girl's cap. She isn't hurrying to sew on those buttons. She has the leisure to look out the window, and it doesn't matter if they are sewn on that day or the next. That's the boy's mother when she was a girl, I'm thinking. Only fine folk have their portraits painted. I want him to know her. It wouldn't be right to claim him as ours."

"Marketday in Groningen tomorrow," Stijn said.

"Oh, no, Stijn. Let's just wait a little."

"We'll be needing money soon."

She slept that night not touching him in the narrow bed. In the morning, she opened the shutters to find ash-gray fog obscuring everything so that she could barely make out their own barn. "Thank you, Heavenly Father," she whispered. Stijn certainly wouldn't send her out on pathless waters in a fog. She'd be sure to get lost. The next marketday, she feigned sickness, but thought he suspected. The next, Piet actually was. In this way the issue of the painting retreated. Often she studied his face, the lines forming around his eyes thin as hairs, to see if he still thought of it.

"How many more potatoes?" he asked one night after the children were asleep.

She knew he meant the eating potatoes, for no farmer, not even a starving farmer, would touch his store of seed potatoes, the new crop Stijn was pioneering in the northland.

"Almost a barrel," she said vaguely.

He didn't ask about the pickled meat. They both knew by her smaller portions that they didn't have much.

"I heard some news on the dike as might interest you."

"What's that?"

"There was a hanging in Delfzijl the day of the flood. A wild witch girl hanged for murder."

"So?"

"So a few days later a baby appears. They always wait for the birth if a woman who's carrying is to hang. Seems to me there's no question."

"This child's mother wasn't a murderer. She wasn't even a shiftless country girl."

"You don't know that for sure."

"Why, just look at the painting. Look at the floor. Stone tiles. Maybe even marble. Look at the tapestry on the table. That's not the home of a wild witch girl, or a peat digger, or even a farmer." She saw his lips press together slightly at her last word. The invention of Jantje's parentage became more real to her as her need for it grew greater. "Jantje came from a good home. In Groningen or Amsterdam. A home with a map on the wall and nice furniture and a mother who wore blue."

"Jantje?"

She flushed when she realized what she said.

"The babe wasn't brought to any other house, Stijn. The Lord has given us a covenant."

"And you break it if you don't sell the painting."

"Can't we just wait? He's not costing us anything. Just a little milk."

"A little milk that would better be going

into cheese. A little milk as could be sold. And don't forget, Katrina'll go dry long before our fields do."

She turned from him. He came up behind her and put his hands on her shoulders. "I'm not asking you to give up the child, Saskia."

She nodded, acknowledging his concession, and stood still to enjoy the weight of his hands. He put his face next to hers and she held her breath.

"Go to Groningen tomorrow. It'll fetch five guilders, surely. Maybe eight if we're lucky. It'll keep us in meat."

"But —"

"See that you shop it around. By the university. Don't accept anything less than eight. Try for ten. And show that paper."

The next morning at dawn, she lowered Piet and Marta, the painting wrapped in a bedsheet, and then the baby into the rowboat. She rowed inland following the bare trees lining the Damsterdiep. The dike road was still under water at first, but farther inland, it slowly began to emerge. Through shallow water pierced by sedges and busy with ducks, she rowed as far as Woldijk, the first dike that held, where it crossed the Damsterdiep. She tied the rowboat to a dike cleat and climbed out, stiff in the legs but feeling the exhilaration of solid ground. She paid a boy half a groat to watch the skiff. Immediately Piet and Marta ran down the dike road crying, "Land, land!" and she let them, until a small barge towed by a horse was ready to leave for Groningen.

The sight of winter fields waiting for planting on the inland side of the dike filled her with hope. But even that wouldn't have the same effect on Stijn. It wasn't hope that lay between that man and God. Nor was it thankfulness. Or appreciation for a bird or a leaf. Or a kiss. Fear lived in that space instead. The horror of seeing the last of the grain and the fields still wet. The fear of having to abandon the farm and starve beside a canal in Amsterdam, the whole family inching forward their alms bowls in front of the poorhouse. But that wasn't the God she cared to know.

In the distance the tower of the church of St. Martin rose above the plain, and as they approached Groningen's tall, stone Water Gate, the children squealed their merriment and jumped up and down. When or where or through what cataclysm do men and women pass that makes them lose that bursting soul-freedom?

They rode past the sugar beet refinery and the metal workers' alley where the children put their hands to their ears, so much banging and hammering there was. To Piet and Marta, Groningen was a dream city, full of magical buildings and arches and windows all containing mysteries. They plagued her with questions — What's that man doing? What's in that cart? What's that metal thing for? — she couldn't keep up with them. And people. So many people, the children marveled.

At the dock Saskia asked directions to the university and entered a stationer's shop full of books and portfolios and papers, some few paintings, and a wealth of detailed drawings of plants and animals and the human body. She laid the painting on the counter and untied the sheet. If she had to do it, she wanted to do it quickly.

The wizened shopkeeper took one look and asked, "Where did you get this?"

She felt Piet and Marta squeeze up against her legs from both sides. "It was given to me." She unfolded the paper for him to see. He held out his hand for it but she wouldn't let it go. She didn't want him to see the back.

As he read, the fingers of his right hand curled in. He gave her a penetrating look, and his eyebrows twitched in a most unpleasant way that made Piet snicker. She squeezed the back of his neck to make him behave. She knew that all the way home in the boat, he'd twitch his eyebrows and then burst out laughing.

The man's gaze crawled down her homespun skirt of black fustian to her old clogs. "Given to you?"

"Yes, sir." She held tight to the paper.

"Do you know who Jan van der Meer is?"

"No, sir."

"I'll give you . . ." he paused, and Marta lay the tips of her fingers along the edge of the man's desk. Saskia shook her head at her slightly, and Marta swept her hands behind her back. "Twenty-four guilders, for it." He turned away and reached for his cash box as if to conclude the deal.

Her surprise made her blurt out, "Twenty-four?" Jantje gave a little cry, and she realized she was holding him too tight. She shifted him from one hip to the other.

"Twenty-five. Not a stuiver more."

Stijn would be jubilant with that. Twenty-five guilders would make him tender to her, and it would make keeping Jantje certain.

But the man wouldn't look at her. He

just sat there stacking up the coins. His fingernails were long and yellow. She couldn't trust a man with long fingernails. The painting must be worth even more. It was certainly worth more than that to her.

"No, thank you." The firmness in her own voice astonished her. Piet gave her a quick look of confusion. She wrapped the painting in the bedsheet, tying the corners carefully, feeling the man following her to the door, his protestations a blur of sound.

Once outside, terror seized her, and she broke out in a sweat. What if she had made a mistake? What if she was only offered less everywhere else? Twenty-five guilders! Besides feeding them until their next crop, twenty-five guilders would buy a sow and a mating hog. Stijn's dream of breeding stock could come true, and she'd be the reason.

"Twenty-five guilders," Piet said with exaggerated authority, and twitched his eyebrows so violently that his whole face quivered. Marta burst out laughing.

Saskia walked briskly but aimlessly through the streets, bought the children a cinnamon waffle at a street cart, and worried. She peered into the window of an antiquarian shop and saw paintings on the wall. She made Marta hold onto Piet and they went inside. Drinking horns and beakers and goblets and tankards stood in a clutter on chests and tables. "Don't touch anything," she warned. Marta and Piet were beside themselves, demanding in whispers that the other one look at each new thing — books, brocade cushions, carvings from the East Indies, and when they found a large mirror, they couldn't resist making faces with their eyebrows, noses, cheeks, lips, everything twitching at once, and giggling at themselves. "Ssh," Saskia commanded, and stifled her own chuckle.

The woman was concluding some business with a man, so Saskia had an opportunity to examine a yellowed, scrolled map hanging on the wall. The place names were all strange. She could find neither Oling nor Westerbork. Her breath leaked thinly out her lungs and she felt that she was from nowhere. Piet and Marta were giggling louder so she pushed them gently to the door and was about to leave when the woman said, "Is there something you might want?"

Saskia started at the sound. "No, thank you," she murmured, and gave an apologetic smile. She paused at the doorway and turned back. "Well, perhaps one thing. Do you happen to know who Jan van der Meer is?"

"Of course. From Delft. The painter from Delft. Vermeer." The woman noticed the painting wrapped in cloth. "You have something to show me?"

Saskia came back in and unwrapped it and the children became serious again. As always when she let herself, Saskia felt sucked into the clean, spare, sunlit room with the young girl in the painting.

"Light. He painted light, you know. Lovely." The woman carried the painting to the window. "Look at her skin. Glazed smooth as silk. Could be. Could very well be."

"Could be what?"

"A Vermeer, my dear."

Saskia unfolded the paper and handed it to her. The woman read it several times, then turned it over. She gave Saskia a long look, then smiled at the baby on her hip.

"Where are you from?"

"Oling. It's only a hamlet. Near Appingedam. We're flooded, and —"

"You take this painting to Amsterdam. It'll fetch a far sight more there than I can pay. Or *anyone* in Groningen. Take it to the shops along the Rokin. Accept nothing less than eighty guilders. And keep it out of the rain."

"Eighty!"

Her voice rose so high that Piet shrieked, "Eighty!"

After more assurances and some shared admiration for the painting, Saskia sold the woman her grandmother's blue linen table scarf with the fine tatting, and then made her way, with the wrapped painting, through the market square to the butchery stalls.

On the row home from Woldijk, her mind flew like a caged sparrow. What would she tell Stijn? That she couldn't sell it? That it only fetched four guilders and so it wasn't worth selling? She'd sell her small spice chest instead. They would get by on that. He'd never know what the first man offered. Or what this woman said. He would trust her. She'd never given him any reason not to.

At home she uncovered the painting and hung it on the peg and put no clothes in front of it. Eighty guilders!

The story she'd imagined came to life for her. Why would such a young woman who could afford to have her portrait painted by a great artist, why would she, how could she have given away her son? She wasn't at peace the way that artist painted her. She was leaning forward, and the rigidness of her spine showed the ache in her soul. She was a desperate woman with frailties just like her, temptations just like her, a woman who had needs, a woman who loved almost to the point of there being no more her anymore, a woman who probably cried too much, just like her, a woman afraid, wanting to believe rather than believing, else why would she give away her son? A woman who prayed, "Lord, I believe. Help thou my unbelief." Saying the words to herself clamped shut her throat and made her cry.

She tried to get the children to go to sleep before Stijn came home. The Lord forgive her or not, she would not tell Stijn. Four guilders, if he asked. After the children were sleeping. Even though the pain of that lie would strike again at the discovery of each new beauty in the painting, truth would drive a wedge between them no tenderness could bridge.

She watched Stijn's eyes when he came in through the window. The first thing he saw was the painting. The second was the pot of beef stew. They hadn't had beef since the flood. She put a bowl of it before him so the aroma would soften him. "I sold grandmother's handworked table scarf," she explained. He took one spoonful standing up and hung his mud-caked reefer on the peg in front of the painting.

She gasped and could barely restrain herself from whisking it away. Marta and Piet poked their heads out from below the cabinet bed. "We saw lots of bridges and churches and beggars," Marta said, and Piet mimicked a blind man holding out his bowl.

"And we rode the towboat," he added.

"Did you, now." Stijn's hand reached down to ruffle Piet's head.

"Ssh. You're supposed to be asleep," Saskia said.

"What about the painting?"

"I'll tell you later," she whispered, motioning with her head to the children. She couldn't lie in front of them.

She watched Stijn eat the stew. When there was only broth left, he tipped the bowl into his mouth. She ladled out more. When he finished, they both stood up at the same moment, both moved one way, then the other to get between the chests and Katrina who swished her tail at the disturbance. Saskia let out a nervous, twittering laugh. He questioned her with his eyes. Earlier than usual, she got into her

131

night shift, blew out the oil lamp, and climbed into the high bed. He showed tremendous patience waiting for an explanation. Only when he lay down next to her did he ask again, "Why didn't you sell the painting?"

"I couldn't," she said, and it was the truth. "I tried," and that, too, was the truth. Let him take it as he would. She rolled away from him. In a moment his hand came across her to turn her again to him. Still he waited.

"Stijn, it's like selling the boy's mother. It's making him an orphan." She knew it was foolish, what she was saying, but in the dark, she could admit things. All the hardness of life in the bleak northland rushed over her like a flood and she cried, "There's nothing beautiful up here. Oh, I know you love it, love to look out on your rows of potatoes, love the big, bare flatness of buckwheat, buckwheat, buckwheat, but I didn't come here for that. I came here because of you, and if we can get along without selling it . . . I'll sell the spice chest. Or we can borrow from Father. The fields will be drained soon. Already at Woldijk you can see sedges coming up through the water."

They lay a long time in the darkness

before he asked, "How much were you offered?"

It was a long time again while she listened for noises from the children. In spite of the quiet, she whispered, "Twenty-five guilders."

He blew air out between his teeth that cooled the back of her neck. She held her breath and didn't move while the enormity of that sum became truth to him. As much as she tried to contain herself, she turned her face into the pillow and cried.

"I would have sold it if I thought that was a fair price."

"Fair? What do we know about such things?"

"I didn't sell it because another woman told me it was worth eighty. In Amsterdam. So you'd best not be treating the painting that way," she said, "hanging your muddy coat in front of it."

"Eighty!" he whispered. After a long, still moment, she felt him get out of bed and heard the sound of him dropping his reefer onto the bare floor.

She had, for the first time in their marriage, a lightness, a sense of power in being right. She pressed further. "As I said, Jantje is not the child of some lawless wench, or even the son of a farmer." She

133

heard the bite in the last word and knew he did too. She turned her back to him and they were both very still until she fell into a sound and peaceful sleep.

In the morning, in those few moments of half-sleep before she moved but when she heard Katrina stirring for her milking, she felt Stijn's arm laid across her lovingly. She lay still to feel the reality of his tenderness, and after a time, she slipped her hand in his.

Work on the sea dikes was completed before they'd expected, and so now all the drainage mills were turning. Stijn worked on the Damsterdiep Dike now, and as the team of men worked their way inland, his spirits brightened. She even saw him tickle Jantje's belly once, and he called him "Jantje" instead of "the baby." Jantje was gurgling baby sounds now. She wasn't sure if she should teach him "Mama" and "Papa," so she was working on "cow" and "water."

If only, for one moment, Stijn could feel as she did, if they could be together in the task God assigned them, if he could look at Jantje as he looked at Piet and Marta and know the power of God's intention, then maybe he'd trust enough to let her keep the painting. But of this, there was no indication. The question of the painting hung in the air of their little upper room, and every day she put less and less salt pork in the stew and then fewer and fewer carrots and haricot beans bought from the vegetable seller who occasionally ventured out to flooded villages in a punt. Eventually the stew became potato broth, day after day, and Saskia thought for sure he'd tell her to sell the painting.

Spring came in small evidences — only a tenderness in the air and some grasses poking the water's surface. Inland, just outside the Woldijk, the land was wet but not flooded, and they were spreading refuse from the city to reconstitute the soil. Farmers there might get their crop of sugar beets after all, but Stijn just sat brooding by the window, looking out at his wet fields. With every week, Saskia pointed out a few more branches of trees emerging and another plank of the barn.

Conscription duties lessened so the Water Board permitted each landowner one day free of dike work each week. There was little Stijn could do on the farm, so he said he'd take them on an outing in the skiff.

"And can we go to Woldijk and have

races on the dike road?" Piet asked.

"Yes, and maybe even to Groningen."

"And see our horse?" Marta added.

"Of course."

It would be a holiday. Stijn hadn't acted this lighthearted in months. She knew there would be heather beyond Woldijk. The marsh gentian wouldn't be out yet, but there would be yellow pimpernel and bog violet she could pick and bring back that would last a day or two. Already the sun breaking through the clouds made the water glisten in silver patches.

But first Stijn went to the barn.

She stood still and closed her eyes. Katrina's endless chewing filled the room.

Across the water she heard him shout. Not words. Not a curse. Just a deep bellow of anguish.

Through the window she watched him thrashing the water with the oars. She had no place to put the older children so they wouldn't see what would come next. She put Jantje far back into their cabinet bed.

Stijn was already yelling as he climbed in the window. "Saskia, how could you? The seed potatoes! You've been using the seed potatoes."

Piet flattened himself against the wall.

"I —"

"Every farm wife knows, every farmer's daughter knows that you don't touch the seed potatoes. There's only a quarter of a barrel left! Not enough to seed more than a few rows of potato mounds."

Marta crawled deep into her bed.

"I thought there was another barrel behind the bales," Saskia said, though she knew, even as she said it, that it was not the truth. They wouldn't get a planting this year so she thought they might as well eat them. The potatoes wouldn't last a year. Now she knew — he hadn't given up the hope of putting in a late crop.

"Another barrel? You knew there wasn't. And you knew if I knew, we'd have to sell the painting."

He didn't lay a hand on her — that he'd never do — but he glared at her with a look that shriveled her soul. She felt God Himself scowling down at her. "Selfish. Selfish! I never knew you."

"Maybe I should tell you then. It was your idea to come up to this barren place. I haven't been back home for three years. My parents haven't seen Piet since he was a baby, but not once have I complained. And not once have I regretted it. And not once have I cursed the flood or bad luck or God Himself. Or you."

"But a man's seed potatoes are his future. It's what he *is*."

"Nothing more? You're nothing more than that? I don't believe it. You're holding a grudge. And you know what? It's not against me, because of the potatoes. Or because I didn't sell the painting. Or even against Jantje. It's because of the flood. And you know who it's against? It's against God. All you see in life is the work. Just planting, hauling, shoveling, digging. That's all life is to you. But not to me, Stijn. Not to me. There's got to be some beauty too."

The upper room was too small to contain him. He climbed out the window, taking Piet and Marta with him, still good for his word to take them on an outing, and she was left with Jantje and Katrina. Their first day outdoors together after more than a year. Ruined. Sobbing, she paced the few steps back and forth across the room, picked up a dried dung cake and hurled it out the window after the retreating boat. It didn't even reach half the distance.

A fine time Piet and Marta would have with that man today. Good riddance to him. She flung herself on the bed so hard Jantje bounced.

Stijn stayed away all day. For the first time during the flood, she was afraid. She'd had a simple faith that everything would be all right — it always was on her family's farm in Westerbork — but Oling wasn't Westerbork. And Stijn wasn't her loving father.

It wasn't that Stijn was unloving. It was just that after eight years, she still had trouble telling the difference between his love and his worry. She'd been wrong about one thing. Stijn's hope. It was there, stronger than hers, but more deeply buried in the dark soil of his soul.

Late in the afternoon she took a good long look, and put the painting in an empty grain sack and sewed it closed.

At dusk she heard the children's voices singing, and his deep voice coming in on the refrain of a silly children's song, but as the skiff drew nearer, the singing faded and eventually stopped. In a sickening silence, Stijn left off the oars and let the boat float slowly toward the house.

Through the window Marta handed her a fistful of wilted blue wildflowers. "Why thank you, *liefje*. These are called lady's smock." She looked at Stijn climbing in after the children. The name meant nothing to him. Piet told her in tumbling sentences all they had done that day, but Stijn was silent. All the anger had gone out of him and only an awkwardness remained.

"I'll go to Amsterdam. The day after tomorrow," she said. "Tomorrow I'll bake enough for you, and I'll take the children. Alda can row me to Woldijk." From there she could get a passenger towboat to Groningen, and another and another all the way to Amsterdam. The trip would take two or three days each way, depending on connections.

On the morning they were to leave, she felt Stijn's eyes as well as Katrina's following her as she packed a few things. "If you can get anything close to eighty," he said as they parted, "take five and buy yourself a different painting. Something you like."

Sitting on the uncomfortable benches on board the large passenger barge headed south from Groningen, she felt like a vagabond surrounded by all that was hers. Occasionally the children's delight at what they saw penetrated her gloom. What was it all for? To have excitement about life, about life together, about a farm and a new kind of crop that would feed the whole world, and then to see it dissolve into only work, work, and tiny, growing separations. How does it all hold together?

Past Assen they had to wait until a lock was vacated by a larger barge, so she got off to let the children run along the dike road. A small waterway led toward the east. "Is that the Westerborker Stroom?" she asked the locksman.

"Aye, ma'am."

Her heart burned. Westerborker Stroom would take her straight through Beilen to Westerbork.

"Does it have service?"

He motioned with his head to a small flatboat waiting to leave.

Just to float home and have Mother feed her something besides potatoes — the mere thought set her in motion. She called to the children, lifted Jantje to her hip, gathered her things and said, "Children, come. We're going to see your grandparents."

They switched to the small flatboat towed by a young man, and sat on the deck leaning up against some crates. New tendrils of willow branches dipped down and floated gracefully. The tall leafy meadow rue was already bursting in fluffy yellow sunbursts, and every duckling peeped his birthsong. Along the banks, the apple trees were in blossom. A breeze blew and ivory petals rained down on the boat and the children tried to catch them. Soon she would be in Westerbork where everything was beautiful and everyone was kind.

Beyond Beilen her heart pounded as the landscape became familiar and her peaceful childhood passed before her. On farmhouse doors she recognized the rustic scenes like she had painted on hers, the only one like it in Oling or Appingedam. Nooteboom's corn mill was painted green now, with a handsome red door. And there was the small stone church she went to as a child, where she and Stijn were married. The sight of it brought a pang of guilt, as if she'd been unfaithful in some way.

At first Mother was delirious with relief and joy, loving the children, Jantje equally with the others, not letting him out of her sight. Saskia thought she knew her mother by heart, but when she showed her the painting and told her everything, her mother's smiles turned hard.

"Seed potatoes! You know better than that."

"I know. I know. May I just stay here for a while, until he gets over it? Long enough so he'll miss me? It's so lovely here. The water violets will be out soon, and the children can run free for a change."

"And let that man worry himself sick over you? No. You leave tomorrow. For Amsterdam. The children can stay with me. Get them on your way back. This isn't a holiday. It's business. And you get down on your knees tonight and thank the Lord you have a man as hardworking as Stijn. Work is love made plain, whether man's or woman's work, and you're a fool if you don't recognize it. The child's the blessing, Saskia, not the painting."

Alone in Amsterdam two days later, she walked along the East Quay past fishwives who shouted insults at her because she passed without buying. She drew her shoulders back. Their mockeries only amused her. While their oily hands were shaking codfish at her, in *her* hands she was carrying a Vermeer.

Spice merchants had set out on the canal edge sacks of powders every shade of yellow and orange and red and brown. Their colors blew onto her skirt and she shook them off. She wore her dainty leather boots with the laces, and she glided along the brickway toward the Rokin feeling a sense of grace and power. She was

143

carrying a Vermeer. The day was sunny. There was no need to hurry.

She walked the Rokin all the way from the Dam to the Singel, keeping the painting in its sack and just looking in all the shops before she declared her business. Art dealers were a strange lot, she decided. Though the signs on the shops identified "Reynier de Cooge, TRADER IN PICTURES," or "Gerrit Schade, EXPERIENCED CONNOISSEUR OF ART," in truth the shops sold frames, clocks, faience, pump organs, even tulip bulbs along with paintings. She showed the painting first to Gerrit Schade, whose walls were covered with scenes of shipwrecks in stormy seas and tavern revels. She suspected he couldn't read. When she held forth the document, he dismissed it with a wave of his hand and offered her thirty guilders.

"It's a Vermeer," she said.

"I don't particularly care for it," he said. "No action. So no drama."

She covered the painting and left.

She would have to be extremely cautious. At the next three shops, she learned to uncover the painting slowly while she watched the dealer's face. At the shop of Hans van Uylenburgh, she noticed at that moment a tiny, sudden intake of breath.

He offered her fifty, and his wife raised it to fifty-five when Saskia shook her head. "MATEUS DE NEFF THE ELDER, only fine paintings and drawings," a sign read. Good. Carefully she held the painting high as she climbed the steep steps. When she uncovered the painting, de Neff made no effort to hide his excitement. "Stunning. Magnificent."

"It's a Vermeer."

"Yes. Yes, it is. A rare find indeed." He called to his associate and his wife to have a look.

She unfolded the paper and he read it carefully, but he spent more time absorbing the painting. "Look at the window glass. Smooth as liquid light. Not a brush stroke visible. Now look at the basket. Tiny grooves of brush strokes to show the texture of the reed. *That's* Vermeer."

She tried to see what he saw but her eyes flooded, and in this last hungry look at the painting, the girl in a blue smock became a blur. She knew she would sell it to him even before he named a price. She wanted it to go to someone who loved it. "I call it *Morningshine*," she softly said. It was important that her name for it go with the painting.

When de Neff was drawing up the document of sale, she looked at everything in his shop. Stijn had said she might buy something inexpensive in exchange. There were paintings of rich people playing lutes and virginals, others of ruined castles in the countryside, kitchen maids scouring pots, church interiors, Noah receiving direction from God, vegetable stalls in marketplaces, and windmills alongside riverbanks. She couldn't choose. Some of them were pleasant. Some were interesting. But none of them *meant* anything to her.

He counted out seventy-five guilders in five florin coins, put them in a muslin drawstring bag, and laid it gently in her hand, supporting the weight with his other hand under hers. Looking softly in her eyes, he closed her fingers over the bag and patted them.

It wasn't eighty, but it was still a victory. They would live. Stijn would have his hogs. Jantje would grow up and help Stijn in the fields, and Stijn would be proud of the work Jantje could do, but they, Saskia and Stijn, would never again be as they were.

She meandered across humped bridges, trailing her fingers lightly over iron railings, bought five tulip bulbs, one for each member of the family, and, while the color of the girl's smock was still vivid in her mind, enough skeins of fine blue Leiden wool to knit a soft woolly for each of her three children.

From the Personal Papers of Adriaan Kuypers

On the day Aletta Pieters was hanged, I came to recognize the tenacity of superstition, even in an enlightened age. And on the day after Aletta Pieters was hanged, in the St. Nicholas flood of 1717, I gave away the only things that mattered to me.

The first time I saw her, she was standing in the pillory of the narrow square in Delfzijl, flinging out curses in a raw voice and spitting at the village boys who were taunting her. None of the matrons glaring at her chastised the boys for their insults. Between two ivory fists, the girl's long hair blew wildly, fine as spun silk the color of nothing, of wind, so light it was, making her seem a creature of exotic plumage caught in a snare. Her eyes, unshielded by any visible eyebrows, had a reckless look. A sly, superior spark leapt from them and fell on me, a stranger shouldering a knapsack and a strapful of books. Her hands relaxed and she teased me with a wanton smile that puckered a small x-shaped scar on her cheek and pushed out her lips across the space between us. I suppose I flushed, for the mark had been laid with precision across the pure beauty of her cheek. The rest of her, hidden by the pillory planks, I could only imagine.

"What did you do against the good people of Delfzijl that you deserve the stocks?" I asked.

"Wouldn't you like to know, now."

The boys hooted a challenge.

"There's more to life than what's in books, Student," she cried. "Come a mite closer and I'll tell ye."

Still with the scholar's close-cropped haircut, I had just fled, disenchanted, from university in Groningen.

"You'd best avert your eyes, lad, if you want it to go well with ye in this town," commanded a weighty matron. "Pack of baggage, she is."

Such virulence did not rest well in this quiet northern village on the Eems Estuary where I had, that day, come to live with my aunt, but the peculiarity of the girl's scar and her wild, colorless hair in brilliant disorder beguiled me. I stepped up to her.

"No spitting," I warned.

"Closer now, don't be afraid. I'll whisper it."

When I bent to put my ear to her face, her hair blew against my cheek like the tingling of fine fresh mist, and she stretched through the pillory hole toward me and licked my ear. "Let that be an omen to ye," she cried.

The boys hooted again, and although I muttered, "Shameless wench," I conceded to myself that my callowness deserved the trick.

The next day, I found her crying on the floor of my aunt's countryhouse in a hump of gray skirt, all the defiance drained out of her. She looked up at a small painting of a young girl about her own age sitting at a window. The flesh of Aletta Pieters's delicate throat had been scraped raw. I crouched beside her. "Is this the same fiery maid as was in the pillory yesterday?" I asked.

She ran sobbing out of the room.

"What's she doing here?" I asked my aunt.

"A year ago the minister found her on the dike road yelling curses, brought her to us filthy and raving, and said, 'The Lord setteth the solitary in families.' He insulted us into taking her. 'Do something decent for God's poor creatures for a change, for the sake of your souls,' he said. So we have to keep her as our wash girl until she's eighteen."

I did not love Aunt Rika, on account of her pretension, but I felt the delicacy of her position, wed as she was, out of love I regret to say, to a slaver, that is, an investor in ships doing Westindische trade, the Middle Passage of which everyone knew but no one acknowledged was in bodies and souls, but passion and prudence are rare sleepmates. Even so, Rika keenly wanted respectability. If she couldn't get it in the sight of God, she'd have to settle for its sham substitute in the sight of man, so while Uncle Hubert attended investors' meetings in Amsterdam, Rika spent well, and gave to the organ society and the orphanage in Groningen. She had filled her townhouse in Groningen with carved furniture and Oriental urns and paintings, and now she was starting on her countryhouse — going to auctions in Amsterdam and hiring an Amsterdammer to paint her portrait with Uncle Hubert.

When Aletta remarked that the face of Rika in the painting was beginning to look like the ghost of the witch of Ameland

Island, Rika got offended and made her sleep in the kitchen and scour the bottoms of all her cooking pans until she could see the "x" on her own face in them. In retaliation, Aletta convinced them by shaking their bed curtains at night that their house was haunted by the souls of dead Africans. One night before I arrived she walked in the fog outside their window with a sheet over her head moaning strange words and clanking pots like a ghost dragging his chains. Uncle Hubert became so terrified he fell out of bed and cracked his skull on the bed steps.

But that wasn't why she was hanged. For scaring him, she only got three days in jail and that one afternoon in the pillory. Before that, she got a beating, two weeks in jail and her cheek slit when a farmer's sluice broke and flooded his field after she murmured something incoherent while passing him in the market square. "I was only playing witches," she'd confessed to Rika. "I meant him no harm." She was pardoned because she was so young, fifteen then, though some townswomen, Aunt Rika said, wished for their sons' sakes that the extremity of the law had been brought down on her then and there.

In truth, she was hanged for smothering our baby girl.

I had come to the village of Delfzijl to study windmill design with the master millwright of the northland. I had worn myself out squeezing some personal meaning out of Descartes, Spinoza and Erasmus and wanted instead to experience in action Descartes's principle that science could master Nature for the benefit of mankind. I wanted the making of practical things — devices to tell time, to pump faster, to see farther — not the making of arguments and treatises. And, I wanted intercourse with flesh and blood, not ink and words.

So the next time I saw Aletta crying in front of the painting, I sat beside her and studied it, trying to understand how something so beautiful could grieve her so. The tenderness of expression on the girl's face showed it was painted with intimacy and love — qualities missing, I supposed, in Aletta Pieters's life. In the painting, the girl's mouth was slightly open, glistening at the corner, as if she'd just had a thought that intrigued her, an effect that made her astoundingly real. To me, she was the embodiment of Descartes's principle, "I think, therefore I am." She was everything

Aletta wasn't — peaceful, refined, and contemplative.

When Aletta finally calmed, I asked her what had made her cry.

"Papa said she had eyes like that, like pale blue moons, and hair like hers, that golden brown color, only in braids. She died when I was born."

"Why don't you braid yours? It might make you feel like her."

"I've tried a hundred times. It just slips out. Nothing holds. It's a curse, I think." The failure made her eyes flood again.

"You have beautiful hair," I said. "Just as it is."

"People think it's false. False hair means bandits will attack soon, and so people hate me."

I turned to hide my smile. "You don't know that for a fact."

She shrugged. The rawness on the curve of her throat had not healed yet. It would be a pity if it scarred, but few there are who go through life unmarked.

"Where is your father?"

"He went to sea on a slaver and never came home."

"Who raised you?"

"Grandfather. My grandmother died young. Same as all the mothers before her.

A mean neighbor put a curse on my Great-great-grandmother Elsa that no girl in her family would ever live long. She said Elsa put *pishogue* on her butter churn and so they tied Elsa's thumbs to her toes and dragged her through the canal and she drowned, so she was innocent. A stork even flew over the canal to prove it."

"There's no such thing as witches or curses, Aletta. You have no proof."

"Oh, there's witches, all right. Grandfather heard them whispering about my mother the night before I was born."

She looked up to the painting imploringly. "You think somewhere girls actually live like that — just sitting so peaceful like?"

Neither a yes nor a no would make her less forlorn. There were no words I could give her to diminish the distance between her and the young woman in the painting.

On Sunday afternoons when I was free from the millwright's instruction, I went walking. I loved the sweep of the flat, domesticated northland that presented few obstacles to wind. Here, most of the time, wind helped man to manage the land scientifically — Descartes in action. I was always bothered, though, that my countrymen depended so completely on its constancy. What would happen if they needed to drain on windless days? There were enormities still to learn in this world.

One Sunday I walked across the peat bog between the town and the coast near where the diggers lived in mean little rows of thatched cottages built of peat blocks. Year after year they dug their slabs of black peat for fuel, and sold their own land, brick by brick, right out from under themselves. Some diggers replaced the overlying clay, mixed it with sand hauled from a beach and refuse from a town to make a soil suitable to grow buckwheat. But it was hard work and took a long time, so others just allowed the pits they had dug to fill with water, leaving straight raised pathways between them. It seemed to me that this practice was only making the land more habitable for frogs, not men. Water was seeping and sucking everywhere. Soon the peat colony would be indistinguishable from the tidal marshes along the great estuary.

I stopped to watch coots poking their beaks into the mud, a teal preening, marsh hens building their nests in the marram grass, and became conscious of a bird call different from the throaty grunt of the coots. It was more like the honk of a wild goose. Across a large pond Aletta had crouched behind some osiers, her skirts hiked up to avoid the mud, baring her legs to her thighs. She wore no knit black stockings like other women, so her milky skin against the mud gave me a pleasurable shock. The sky was too gray to give back an inverted figure in the pond water, which I thought a shame. With her hands cupped at her mouth, she made the bird call again, urgent and wild and yearning. My soul stirred with the stirrings of her hair. I meant to walk on and enjoy my solitude, but an inner movement seized me and I circled the pond and came up behind her.

"What are you doing?" I asked.

"Get down," she whispered, and yanked my arm. "I saw a stork here the other day, and I want to see if he'll come again. They bring good luck, you know. If you can get one to eat out of your hand, you'll never go hungry."

I snickered.

"Don't laugh at something you don't know about, Student. If one nests on your roof, you'll get rich. I know. I grew up on Ameland Island."

My amusement at the simple certainties of her universe inflamed the little "x" on her cheek. She let down her skirts, tugged her sea-colored shawl around her, her proud breast rising and falling in pique, and walked off a ways, her pretty pout pushing out her lips. "You've ruined it now, you noisy boy."

"Then come with me for a walk."

She didn't move so I went on by myself, disappointed. Soon I saw a white bird wading on long black legs. "Aletta," I called. "Here's a stork."

She came crashing through the marsh grass splashing us both with muddy water. "Oh, that's only an old spoonbill. No black wing feathers. No red legs." She followed me now along the thread of pathway near the diggers' colony.

The deckhouse of a sailing barge protruded above the dike of the Damsterdiep on its way to deliver peat to Groningen. "What's going to happen when they dig up so much peat that their own houses sink into the bog?" I asked.

"Move somewhere else."

"You don't get the point. There has to be a better way."

"Meantime, they've got to live." She pulled out some osiers right in front of someone's cottage and used them to whisk the air free of insects as we walked. She was close enough now that I smelled her blown hair salted with sea wrack.

We followed the Damsterdiep under the elms. She fascinated me with dark stories her grandfather told her, about shipwrecks and sailors and women cursed to sail with them forever, never putting foot on land, but tied to bowsprits when the ships came into ports. Her great-great-grandfather, she claimed, was the lighthouseman, Varick, of the Ameland light across the Wadden Sea. He got rich, she said, by sending out false signals so trading ships would run aground in the shallows and he'd collect their goods in a skiff or wade out at low tide and pick them up. She told it without shame, and with what I took to be an admiration for his cleverness. She told how sailors' wives made a healing froth by soaping the skull of a person who died violently, mixing it with two spoonsful of human blood, a little lard, linseed oil and some Java cinnamon. She showed me a nutshell she wore on a string filled with spiders' heads to ward off fevers. I saw only the smooth skin on which the nutshell rested. When she cautioned me to place my shoes upside down at night like she did to frighten away witches, I laughed, which made her eyes narrow and reveal a darker spirit. Although it all struck me as quaint and engaging, I could see that the poor girl was haunted by a hundred demons.

At the drawbridge over the Damsterdiep I stopped to study the mechanism. Bridges, windmills, locks and dikes had fascinated me since boyhood, and I marveled out loud how they all worked together in a system of integrated parts.

"It doesn't matter how they work," she said. "When the waterwolf wants to come up over those dikes, he's going to, and no pile of mud and seaweed is going to stop him."

I was undaunted. We crossed the Damsterdiep, and at the Farmsum mill, with the miller's permission, I showed her how drainage mills worked. In the province of Groningen they were mostly screw mills, lifting water on an enormous, sheathed Archimedean screw placed at an angle below water level in a deep ditch. She had never been inside a windmill before and so she stood astonished and kept her arms crossed over her chest, afraid to touch anything. When she grasped how the movement of the sails turned each connected part of the mechanism, it gave me a surprising, indescribable happiness.

In explaining it, I realized that the wind shaft wheel had sixty-eight teeth, and the connecting gear post had thirty-four staves at the top wallower as well as at the bottom crown wheel, and the connecting gear at the head of the Archimedean screw had thirty-four also. That meant that for every turn of the sails, the screw turned twice. If its head was made to have only seventeen staves, I reasoned, wouldn't that mean that the ratio would be one turn to four, and the land could be drained twice as fast? Or with half the windpower? And if the spiral blade on the screw could be wider, that would increase the uptake of water on each turn.

"Not so fast," the miller said. "You've got to consider what wind power 'twould take to lift more water."

We talked at length while Aletta went off following a duck and her ducklings in the drainage ditch. As a result we got caught in the rain coming home. Rain bubbled up in puddles on the bricks of the square, and where the bubbles broke, Aletta would not step across them even though she wore *klompen*. It would profane the breath of God to be released up her skirts, she said, her eyes widening in a gravity I found enchanting.

When we came home together, wet to the skin, Rika took me aside. "You'd best mind yourself with that girl, Adriaan. Not a speck of sense. She'd walk over one night's ice on a dare. You get mixed up with her and you'll be finding another aunt to house you. If Hubert were here, he'd say the same."

Church towers, windmill caps, dike roads all afforded views of the flat expanse around Delfzijl. Nothing was hidden, and that made everybody's business everybody else's, which was, I realized, just the way they liked it. Rika even kept her curtains open as a display of virtue. The only place Aletta and I could be together unseen was just under the rafters in the church tower, a circumstance that propelled us into an earlier intimacy than what we would have known had we been permitted to walk together Sunday afternoons under the wide sky. Using the church as a refuge was her idea. Since the bell was rung from below, we wouldn't be discovered, and the church was never locked, she said. I liked her contempt for conventional piety, yet she had a personal code as rigid as any Calvinist's.

Elevation in a land so flat was a heady feeling, one that nudged aside caution and gravity and worship. Above the narrow strip of the village we felt like stowaways on a ship bound for some pleasure isle that the good people of Delfzijl feared even dreaming about lest the mere thought would sweep them into hell. With her I was in another world, drawn into her being. It became impossible to read in the evenings. The sound of her girlish voice moved me now as surely as the silent voices of sages had months earlier, and her smell of blacksoap and sweat sent me into tremors of excitement.

Under the holy rafters she met my shy, formal advances step for step, accompanied by grateful, urging noises, until one spring afternoon in the dark church, a flood threatened to crash over me. I drew apart and she laughed in a way that made me feel childish. I gave a little tug to the drawstring on her chemise and discovered, by accident, that she carried a lucky bean between her breasts. I leaned her backwards and kissed the two pink ovals of warm flesh where the bean had pressed. Beneath the layers of gray skirts she wore, she arched up to meet me, pressing, urgent, beyond all bearing. Her thighs opened, and I was lost to any Heaven but Aletta. Aletta. *Aletta.*

Afterward, I expected her eyes to have a misty distance, searching to see if she needed to feel ashamed. Instead, she straightened her clothing, and said, "Well, so it's done then."

"What's done?"

"You mean to marry me."

Her simplemindedness knocked all breath out of me. I didn't say anything, yea or nay. I didn't have to. Her faith in the bean assured her of whatever she wanted to think. The morning I was to show the millwright my drawings of a better mill design, I found it in my breeches pocket. It was the same bean for sure, with speckles, an enormous sacrifice. I was about to throw it away when some tenderness made me put it back in my pocket. It seemed a sort of proffered pledge.

One night not long afterward at Rika's house, Aletta heard a loud scraping sound and then a crash. She tore through the rooms looking for the reason, and when she found the painting of the girl having fallen off the wall, she screamed and backed away, her breast heaving, and her hands pulling at her hair. Aunt Rika, Uncle, everyone was roused, and Rika made her drink hot milk to calm her. I showed her that the broken cord on the back of the painting had come untwined, but still she would not be consoled. "You watch. Something terrible is going to happen." Nothing quieted her until I folded her in my arms, which told Rika rather more than I'd intended.

The next morning, Rika followed me outdoors as I left for the millwright's. "There's nothing of the Holy Spirit in her, Adriaan."

"You're wrong, Rika. There's nothing but spirit. With such demons chasing her, it's by God's grace alone that she even has faith enough to take a breath." I turned and left, that spirit potent over me as an act of nature.

Our plan for the birth had been to wade at low tide across the Wadden Sea to Ameland Island where she had some rights of inheritance. No one lived in the big house except her deaf old grandfather and his housekeeper. We could stay there until we decided what to do, but it was late November and a gale brought driving rain and we couldn't cross or even get a herring boat to take us there, and so she made it look like she'd run away, but I knew where she was.

Secretly, a little at a time, she had brought up to the church tower dry straw, a blanket, water, bread, candles and an old

165

basketful of clean rags. Every day as we waited for her time to come, I brought her a crock of ale from the tavern and food that I stole from Aunt Rika's kitchen. She asked for buttered bread and ewe's milk cheese to swallow right after the birth, and, to wrap up with the child, she wanted a cabbage leaf in case of a boy and a clump of rosemary in case of a girl. Out of fear to set her raging, I complied. By then, I'd do anything she told me to.

I even watched when she poured molten wax into a bowl of water. When the drops hardened, she laid them in a row to study their shapes. Her face twisted into a torture of grooves and she swept them up in her fist.

"Well? What's it mean?" I asked, ashamed at my own curiosity about what was only folklore.

"Can't tell you. It'll make it true if I tell you."

It infuriated me that she wouldn't say. I had lost hold of reason, of all that I'd believed to be true.

She refused a midwife even though I pleaded with her. She said midwives in Delfzijl were all under oath to report any illegitimate births to the town council, who might take the child, so I had to do it myself. When it was time, she signaled me by hanging out her shawl from the stone grating up under the eaves and I made some excuse to the millwright and came across the square in the rain. I found her gripping the rafter above her head. "Now don't you pass out dead cold at what you see," she said. She told me what to do and I did it. Once she had said she'd never been made love to by a man before me, yet she had an exact knowledge of birthing, and she wasn't the least bit afraid, which made me wonder, just before the baby came, if it really was her first.

I felt weak with the magnitude of what was before me — the blood, the smell — and what I was holding in my hands — quivering life. "A fine, healthy boy," I managed to say. Aletta only moaned. I cleaned him up, set him in the basket and had my hands out ready for what she said would slide out next, when she screamed again, the sound muffled by pounding rain. She gave a mighty heave and out came another head. Shaking, I supported it in the palm of my hand.

Twins were the worst kind of omen, Aletta said afterward, and this one, her little lip was split like a cat's or a hare's. "The mark of the Evil One's claw on her surely."

"That's nothing of the kind," I said, with less firmness than I had intended.

I had no choice but to make her as comfortable as possible and go back to Rika's.

The next day, when I brought her midday supper, Aletta said the girl couldn't suck without the milk coming out her nose. "She'll live a short life taunted by jeers and she'll turn mean and wild and then die of loneliness. Better dead already. Better send the poor thing to her Maker before she gets used to life."

"Aletta, don't you be thinking such a thing."

I was afraid to leave her, but I had to go home to avoid suspicion. "You lay one hand against that child and you'll endanger your immortal soul." I gave her a hard look and told her not to move from that spot until I came tomorrow. I lay awake all night listening to thunder crack the world.

Hard, driving rain beat on the roof of the millhouse where I worked the next morning on a windmill model, carving a drainage screw with a small gear head and wider blades. I prayed the rain would continue and drown out any babies' cries that villagers might hear. With more food for her and some milk, I slipped in the side door of the church, tasting the rank odor of mildew, and climbed the wooden stairs in an agony of dread.

The boy was at her breast, her hand behind his little skull. The basket was empty.

"Where's the girl?"

Aletta, with bitten, swollen lip, fixed on me a fierce glare. "You breathe one word of this, Adriaan, and they'll stretch a rope around my neck surely."

"My God, Aletta."

"What do you know, Student, about a mother's rights?"

"What about a father's?"

"You didn't read the wax drops, Adriaan. I had no choice."

"Tell me where she is, Aletta."

She turned her face away. I looked at her hands and saw dirt under her fingernails. Mud had smeared her skirt, her elbow and her cheek.

"Tell me where."

Her stony coldness was more convincing of the cataclysm than the dirt. Argument was as futile now as blame in Eden. I could not bear to look at her. She had cast away her soul.

Even in this, nature worked against her: She didn't dig deep enough and rain washed away the loose dirt. The next day townswomen discovered the poor sodden babe in the mud. That sent the aldermen straight to Rika, and my honest aunt told them Aletta had run off. It wasn't long before they would find her, I knew. In the righteous town of Delfzijl, iniquity was as unable to be hidden as a windmill on a mudflat. "Look in the mills. Look in the barns. Look in the church. She's bound to be somewhere," Aunt Rika told Alderman Coornhert, and then she gave me a look of righteous defiance.

A few hours later, Aletta burst through the doorway shrieking, "Adriaan! Mistress! Don't let them take me." Fighting the aldermen who seized her, she cried out to me, "Don't let them foam my scalp. Don't let them, Adriaan. I'm warning you." She leveled at me a look that paralyzed me, but no one seemed to notice me, and whatever I said was lost amidst her arms flailing against their chests and her hair whipping their faces. They had who they wanted.

I stood dumb and helpless before the door a long time after they left.

"You only think you love her now, Adriaan," Rika said softly. "There will come a time, though you can't imagine it now, when you will not be able to remember her face."

I looked at Rika with her braid wound smugly on the top of her head, not a hair disordered. "You don't know what you're talking about."

I had two beautiful days with the baby in the bell tower. Several times a day and throughout the rainy night, I soaked a corner of Aletta's shawl with ewe's milk I got from the millwright's boy and let the baby suckle it the way I'd seen a farmer do with an orphaned lamb, with his little finger in the lamb's mouth. I did the same, though I didn't know how to hold him properly. I tried to remember how Aletta did. When he was satisfied, his wiggly arms flew open, and his blue eyes closed to slits. It fairly split me with joy when his tiny dimpled fist with fingernails like flakes of candle wax performed his first miracle: He grasped my index finger.

By the third morning the babe seemed listless. Gnawing hunger had set in. While I fed him again, the truth I had resisted became clear: I would have to give him to someone who could mother him. I wrapped him in clean rags, settled him warmly in the basket hidden in the bell tower and left to search for someone. It occurred to me as I walked that Descartes had a child by his maidservant in Amsterdam. But Descartes got to raise his child as his own. No house in Delfzijl had a small wooden placard covered with red cloth hanging under the eaves announcing a new baby in the family, but what did it matter? If he were suspected to be Aletta's baby, no one would take him.

At the next feeding, I found a way to dribble milk down my finger into the baby's mouth and I think he got more that way, but time was short.

In a chilly mist, I crossed the slippery Damsterdiep Bridge to Farmsum. Along the way the men of the Water Boards of Delfzijl and Farmsum were measuring seepages and stamping on the ground, and farmers were building cofferdams in suspect places. There were no new birth placards in Farmsum. I returned to feed the baby and then went inland under a steady drizzle along the shores of the Damsterdiep, to Solwerd, crossing fields spongy with eight days of rain. There, farmers were building earthen animal ramps and hoisting stores on block and tackles from gable beams into upper rooms and barn lofts. No birth placards in Solwerd either. I would have gone all the way to Appingedam but Rika would have asked me where I was if I weren't home for supper. I fed the babe again and came home soaked. Since Uncle Hubert was in Amsterdam, Rika asked me to haul her ornate mahogany spice chest upstairs. Even with all forty-eight drawers taken out, I could barely manage it myself, and fell into bed exhausted.

I wrestled through the night in wakeful darkness. Aletta Pieters was to hang at noon the next day. If I went to watch, I would live with the horror the rest of my life. If I didn't, I would be forsaking her. Better memory than betrayal, I decided.

A noon hanging was sure to attract a crowd, so if I went and joked with the village lads in front of the Raadhuis, no one would suspect, but when the church tower struck eleven and rain began again, I entered the square and found it empty. If I were the only watcher, that would declare me the father for sure. But that wasn't the reason I kept walking. I just couldn't bear so close a view. In an act of supreme cowardice, I crossed the square and climbed the church tower. From the window grating in the bell tower I could see the Raadhuis where they'd raised the gallows. Maybe she'd look up here.

The deadened thump of rain on roof tiles grew to a roar that I hoped might drown out the noon chime. At the half-chime, puddles had joined to become great pools, and men headed out across the peat bogs with their carts loaded with huge willow mats and boards, slabs of turf and sacks of sand, shovels and stakes and lanterns on poles. Flood was on everyone's mind, so no one came to see Aletta Pieters hang. The only townspeople left were the presiding aldermen and the sheriff, women trying to get their cows upstairs, girls carrying bedclothes and stores of food and peat into attics, and small boys securing skiffs by long ropes to roof beams.

When the cart rolled up, she was strapped to a post, her arms bound to her sides. She had no hair at all! Bitter anger exploded in my throat. Someone had shaved her. Preparation for frothing, she'd think. It was probably only the jailer's wife wanting her hair for its strange color to weave it into belt buckles. Anyone who tried to would be cursed in the attempt. Aletta's silky hair would never hold.

Awkwardly, I held the babe face out in front of me. His first view of the world out the window would be to see his mother hang. How much he had to learn. I draped a corner of Aletta's shawl out the window to tell her we were watching, and prayed she would see it. I think she stood up straighter on the cart just then and stretched her neck longer, as though Rika herself were watching her. The shame of dying, of being sent to die, was nowhere in her posture. She scanned the skies. I hoped, in all that grayness, she might see a stork. Or a bubble bursting that might tell her God was breathing all around her. Her dripping gray dress clung to her and showed the small, beautiful mound of her stomach. I swallowed back the closest thing I knew to love.

Rain pelted the bricks in the square, smacked against the windows and ran down in sheets. No doubt all those windows along the square had gawking faces in them cursing the rain for obscuring the view. Alderman Coornhert strode back and forth like a general under the stepped eaves of the Raadhuis behind a fringe of water. Get on with it, man! Petty arm of provincial justice. Can't offend anyone by enacting its judgments too soon, or too late, or not at all. Order. Order must be had. Though the water-soaked earth be removed and though the mountains be cast into the sea, order must be had. They would hang her punctually at noon, making her wait that last miserable half hour in bone-chilling rain, her head shaved. The defenselessness of her quivering, swollen lip should have shamed them into some kind of mercy, even that of a sooner death than noon.

Close behind me in the tower the great bell sounded. The baby jerked in my arms. I held him tighter. Then again, the bell resounded in my chest on its slow, pompous way to twelve peals.

Would Aletta have appreciated the totality of effect — the air gray with rain, and the gibbet and the plain stone Raadhuis behind just a darker gray — if she had been watching this from a different perspective? Would she have noticed rain pouring off the ends of her fingers, elongating them into liquid gray roots like witches' hands?

I'd look at her hands, only her hands, even though I couldn't see where the fingers stopped and the rain began. Rain poured off them until that sudden unmistakable jolt, which I did see, will always see, when her feet kicked wildly, kept kicking, her *klompen* flying off, and in my mind's eye, her hands flung the water away, and in another moment rain poured

176

off her hands and her still feet smoothly again in slender silver ropes.

My soul shuddered.

I turned my back to the window and bowed my head over the babe until the echo of the twelfth chime had died. "Father, give Thy benediction, give Thy peace before we part," I whispered, my breath moving the baby's feathery hair. "Peace which passeth understanding, on our waiting spirits send."

Behind closed eyes I saw again the jolt, the flung water, her feet, wild then still.

Anyone standing close enough to be wet by the flung water, she might have said, ought to expect some bad luck having to do with water, the least of which might be burning one's mouth to shreds with hot tea, the greatest, drowning in the flood that was sure to come. The curse of the flung water, she'd call it.

Quick peals of alarm followed. I nestled the babe in the basket, left him in the tower and stumbled down the narrow stairs hardly able to see, to join the few remaining townsmen running across the peat bogs. Blown rain needled my face and I slipped and fell. All along the Damsterdiep, windmills had stopped with their vanes in the alarm position.

Wind-whipped peaks sloshed over the sea dike in places. Gray, impersonal death was licking at the continent. The waterwolf of Aletta's nightmares was baring white fangs that dripped their foam over the embankment. I joined the lines of men working to raise the crown of the dike with planks. Between each plank, I shoveled clay like a madman.

Late in the afternoon, to the north, where no one was working, the sea folded over the dike and gushed across the lower peat bogs, filling in the pits. We climbed the dike slope to work above waterline until a skipper in the estuary steered his scow broadside into the breach and we could secure it with ropes and pack the gaps with seaweed, reed mats and slabs of turf. Then the sea broke through another place. Loss swept over me, and for a moment I couldn't get my breath. Probably all along the coast, the sea was winning.

We mended the new gap with the side of the nearest barn torn down, secured it with ropes to dike cleats, and tamped clay against it. In quickly fading light, I could see the patched place bowing. All night in glassy blackness we lay with our heels dug into the upper incline of the dike and braced it shoulder to shoulder, our arms linked in a numb chain and our backs pressed up against the slanted dike wall. The wolf on the other side sprayed icy sea-water on my sweating face, and my arms burned. I closed my eyes against the pain and imagined Aletta walking a sinuous path to avoid bubbles in puddles. Rain fell down the back of my neck and rain was falling on the church tower and the Raadhuis and the gallows and Aletta's unprotected head. Inland I could see a row of watch fires stretching far to the north. I counted them, and later counted them again, and when there were fewer, I knew the sea had broken in somewhere else. The land would be covered. Thunder and wicked lightning bore wave after wave of shock and disbelief and anger until all shock and anger and disbelief were washed out of me and there was only shivering loss. And the babe in the tower hungry and crying through the night.

Eventually we could feel and hear that the tide had turned. Whatever water would come had come already. Slowly shapes began to emerge, the rain thinned to a silver mist, and there was a kind of horrific beauty in the muted dawn. Stepping away from the incline, I stood like a crucifix, unable to lower my arms. In milky gray light, I turned and saw that the fleshy forearm I'd been gripping all night was Alderman Coornhert's.

"You're a fine lad," he said. "Far better'n the likes of her."

Rage hissed through me. Who else had known?

I jostled a place in the first punt back to Delfzijl. Peat bogs and farms were all under water. Bare trees were only bushes of twigs now. Families of peat diggers waited on soggy thatched roofs or shared tree branches with chickens. A miller's family huddled on the cap of the mill. Big, gentle Groningen draft horses swam mutely, aimlessly, without understanding. I envied, for a moment, the simple griefs of animals.

Without the straight lines of canals and ditches outlining farmers' plots, there was less of a human mark upon the land. The town was shortened, diminutive. In Delfzijl, water flooded the just and the unjust. Only the lower rooms of houses were under water. And the church floor. The babe was safe in the tower, I knew. We floated through the square between the Raadhuis and the church, the water as flat as a pewter plate, upon which an enormous rat rode a wooden door. An omen,

Aletta would have said. But the gibbet and Aletta Pieters had been washed away.

Aunt and Uncle's house was scaled down, humbled by the water at window level on the lower floor. From the punt, I climbed through a half-submerged window and found Rika, wet from the waist down, on the stairway, in one arm a Ceylon urn, in the other the painting of the girl, each one acquired by sending a soul to hell on earth in the Americas. No human being tied me to Rika's house decorated by oppression, or to this town of quick and simple justice. Redemption earned through the begrudged boarding of an orphan was too easy. I needed to return to more diffi-cult ideas.

"You look like —"

"I have to leave, Aunt."

"Yes, you do. I'm surprised you stayed to help."

"You know?"

"Missing girl. Missing food. Nephew out all hours. Sits in an empty church like some Catholic. I expected you to leave when they — at noon yesterday."

"You knew she was in the church, and you sent them there!"

"To save you from her."

"Save me?"

"You're free," she stammered shame-fully.

How could I explain to one who thought like that?

"Rika, I need money."

"Money?" She set the urn on a step and gave me a puzzled look. "Half the country-side under water and you're worried about money?"

"There was a second child."

She inhaled a loud, exaggerated breath and made me wait for her answer. "If I give you something, will you promise to take the child away?"

"You think I'd leave him to the good people of Delfzijl?"

"Take this." She held forward the paint-ing. "Sell it in Amsterdam. I'll give you the dealer's paper. It was her favorite, despite her tears." Her chin quivered. "I can't enjoy it anymore."

"My mill drawings?"

"I saved them too. Upstairs."

"Give them to the Water Board."

Through waist-high water I followed her upstairs and took the painting, the paper, another blanket, my books and knapsack, a cheese quarter Rika handed me, loaded Uncle Hubert's skiff and pushed off. Rika stood at the upper window as if on a houseboat, or an ark. "Remember, Rika," I said, "when the Lord repented for having made man, He brought the flood."

I climbed into the church loft, changed the baby's rags, fed him, wrapped him in Aletta's shawl and blanket and laid him in the stern of Uncle's skiff so I could see him, propped the painting and my knapsack next to him and covered the whole with another blanket like a tent. Exhausted, I pulled away from the town of Delfzijl and its muddy truths.

At first, swirling water mastered me, and the current of the Damsterdiep carried me backwards until I learned to recognize it rippling the surface, and navigated near farmhouses to avoid it. My arms cramped and I had to let go of the oars from time to time, and my ears ached from cold air blown across them.

Inland, toward Solwerd, the waters calmed, and the rhythmic motion of the boat cradled the babe to sleep. Wind drove an opening in the clouds, and the sun cast a silver glare over the water. Past Solwerd, watery desolation spread out in a dreadful, false calm. When the land was drained, the fields would be covered with sea sand, and the soil would be salted for years. All my pride at science mastering nature was swept away. Time was sporting with man. My faster pump mill was years too late, and Aletta and I were years too early.

"Far better than the likes of her" wasn't true. I hadn't fought off any demons. I had just drifted with her currents, while she. . . . Never did she succumb to the cowardice of self-pity. I had fancied love a casual adjunct and not the central turning shaft making all parts move. I had not stood astonished before the power of its turning. All I'd learned at university to be firm and eternal was floating unanchored, and, as a result, God seemed much less scrutable on the long row back.

Appingedam was under water too. I reached it by midafternoon. People were out in skiffs rescuing animals and goods before the early dark. Past it, in the hamlet of Oling, two young children leaning out a red-shuttered upper window waved to me and called out, "St. Nicholas! St. Nicholas," laughing.

"Have you any milk?" I called.

They only giggled. I asked again, and they disappeared below the sill. Above the water, I could see that the door, arched over by a leafless vine, was painted with a rustic scene the way country people do farther south. In a few moments a woman

184

came to the window and lowered down a wooden bucket with an earthenware jar of milk inside. I picked it out, thanked her and rowed on out of view behind a barn and tied up to a tree. I soaked my sleeve in the milk and dripped it into the baby's mouth.

I regretted that I didn't know any lullabies. All those mothery sounds one makes for babies — I knew none of them, and all I could think of was the doxology.

"Praise God from whom all blessings flow," I softly sang, letting the milk flow into his mouth and smiling at him.

"Praise Him, all creatures here below."

The woman had asked no questions before she brought the milk to the window. A knot swelled in my throat. Those were happy children in the window. Here was the place.

"Praise Him above, ye Heavenly Host."

This first time would be the last time I'd sing to my little son. My voice cracked in a thin whistle.

"Praise Father, Son, and Holy Ghost."

At dusk, a man rowed a skiff toward the house, tied it to the gable, handed a flapping chicken through the window, and then climbed through himself. I dug into my knapsack for a pencil stub and on the back of the art dealer's document, I wrote, "Sell the painting. Feed the child," and wrapped my son, the paper and the cabbage leaf in the blanket. Lulled to a sitting sleep by exhaustion and the lap of water against the hull, I woke in darkness and placed our beautiful son in the man's skiff, sheltering him with the painting and the blanket, and took to my oars.

Pulling away, I heard the boat nudging the house in timid little wave surges, as if knocking politely, like a blessing, and I knew that I would row all the way back to Groningen, if need be, until I could feel solid ground under me once more.

And for this return, I wonder, would it be blasphemy to thank God?

Adriaan Kuypers, College of Science and Philosophy, Groningen University, St. Nicholas Eve, December 5, 1747. Rain all day.

Still Life

In the stately brick townhouse of Pieter Claesz van Ruijven on the Oude Delft Canal, Johannes was welcomed into the same wood-paneled anteroom where he'd come to offer his paintings, one by one, over the past ten years.

"He is occupied at present," the young servant said. "What shall I tell him is the nature of your business?"

"I was hoping to see the paintings."

A quick, two-note giggle escaped her. "You? You haven't seen them enough already?" She ushered him into the great hall. "I'll tell him you're here."

Left alone. Exactly what he'd hoped for. His paintings warming the room from all sides.

View of Delft, large and alone and radiant on the far wall. Morning's breathless stillness before the city wakes from within. Light the only actor, streaming down lovingly onto the far tower of Nieuwe Kerk and the orange roofs in the city's distance.

And in the foreground the town wall, Schiedam and Rotterdam Gates and even the herring boats, all still, darker, under a cloud, not yet waking. In such momentary quietness, would anyone else ever feel the grace of God? To see the painting from this distance, he could take it all in at once. Walking toward it as if approaching the city thrilled him. He'd never experienced that sensation in the small upper room across the river he had rented to paint the view.

Oh, for that room again. For its gift of silence. Now he painted in the main room of his family's cramped lodgings right on the market square. Eleven children were always running underfoot, their *klompen* clattering on the tile floor. The boys screaming their imaginary battles. The girls bickering over chores. Little Geertruida's tortured coughing. The baby crying. His mother's boisterous tavern just next door, and Willem, his besotted brother-in-law, shouting wild claims through the passageway.

He craved quietness. Any abrupt noise could make him take a stroke at the wrong angle; then light wouldn't fall correctly on the grooves left by the brush hairs; he'd have to stroke over it again. With that extra layer of paint, the mistake would be raised from its surroundings by the width of a silk thread. That he could not disguise. Every time he looked, there it would be, screaming at him. Failures like that would paralyze him if he saw any today.

Instead, he scanned the painting for places of splendid exactitude, marks of authority of his brush. Here, up close, there was comfort in the glazed smoothness of the blue slate roof of the Rotterdam Gate, and rightness in the sanded texture of his impasto on the foreground roof tiles. Yes. But were these only accidental successes?

Something in the great hall felt different. He looked around. Ah! Pieter had moved *Little Street* adjacent to *View of Delft*. He liked that proximity, the dear, quiet commonness of *Little Street* next to the grandness of the whole city. He felt as a quickening in his blood the absolute, startling necessity of the Venetian red shutter on that little street, and the intimacy of the figures quietly going about their lives. A girl knelt at the curb, her back to the viewer so that her raw umber skirt ballooned out behind her like an enormous, airy pumpkin. It pleased him all over again. He'd seen his own girls sit just like that, utterly and happily engrossed.

But did the world need another painting of people quietly going about their lives? Could another painting make up for the scarcity of meat on his family's table?

Behind him boot heels clicked against the marble floor. He turned and asked, "How goes it with you, Pieter?"

"Fine. Fine."

"The brewery?"

"Excellent well. Rising as surely as the head on a good ale." Pieter offered him a glass of wine from a bulb-shaped white decanter. Jan held up his hand to decline. "So you have begun another painting and have come to entice me with the hearing of it?"

"No new painting just yet. I'm trying to decide."

"Just pick one of those daughters of yours or Catharina again, set her down, and paint. Your brush will do it."

In a loud puff of breath Jan vented his amusement at Pieter's simplicity.

"I know you think it's got to embody some truth," Pieter said in an exaggerated, plodding rhythm, smiling.

"Or if not, then at least give compensation for reality."

For a painting to say something he held

to be true, it took rumination, sometimes months of apparent inactivity. He could not will himself to discover truths. But he could give himself over to a painting or a subject with devotion and ardor, like the girl was doing nosing down onto that curb, committing body and soul to her endeavor. Yet now he felt hesitant before any subject that suggested itself, flogging himself with the sin of selfishness if he were to continue.

"A man has time for only a certain number of paintings in his lifetime," Jan said. "He'd better choose them prudently."

"You will. I know that. You like to make me wait."

Jan chuckled gravely, knowing he was being teased. He felt himself wrestling with the imminent maw of nonpainting he was not sure would still be life. Whenever he approached the completion of a painting he could sense a shameful dread of resuming contact with the realities of hearth and family. His family receded into vagueness while he was deeply at work on a painting, but between paintings, it advanced into sharp responsibility.

"I've been given the opportunity to enter the caffa cloth business with a cousin," Jan said. "I know something about it. My father was a caffa weaver."

Pieter lit his arched porcelain pipe. Through the smoke his expression became solemn. "You have another obligation, you know."

Yes, he knew. The two hundred guilders Pieter had advanced him against the sale of his next two paintings, whether to Pieter or to anyone else. Yet now he needed two hundred more. "I know, I know. I'm looking for a subject."

"I don't mean the debt. I mean a deeper obligation. The obligation of talent."

Yes, speak of that, he said to himself. Convince me. He regarded the glowing yellow-ochre light streaming over the hands of *Girl Reading a Letter at an Open Window.* "Why does the world need another painting of a woman alone in a room? Or a hundred more paintings?"

It was a risk to say that. Maybe he'd made a mistake, but he was desperate for Pieter to give him an answer to counter his self-doubt, that shadow companion that lay each night between Catharina and him in the darkness, scraping raw his need to be in the security and joy of the next painting.

"The world doesn't know all that it needs yet," Pieter said, "but there will come a time when another of your paintings of a woman by a window will provide something."

"But the cost . . ." And he didn't mean the price he would set. The cost was to his household. The cost was to Catharina who never had him fully to herself. Any anticipated private moment with him was invaded by his intimacy with a painting. The cost was to his little Geertruida, who, through lack of a winter's cloak or a proper fire, suffered a lingering sickness. Every painting, every month he did not work at selling cloth cost his family something.

"So if not to tell me of a new painting, then what, Master Jan?"

"I —" Suddenly, what he really came to ask congealed on his tongue and he could not bring it out. "I just came to study the paintings."

"Any time, my good man." Pieter slapped him on the back. "Any time. The hall is open to you. And now, if you'll excuse me . . ." He stepped to the double doors and then turned back. "Paint, Johannes, paint."

Jan smiled and nodded at Pieter. No one but another painter could know the delicacy required to balance the complexities, to keep reality at bay in order to remain in the innermost center of his work, without which he knew he would only exist at the periphery of art, a mere provincial painter. Limited output and limited following.

One by one, he assessed the rest of his paintings, nine in just this hall, drinking in like a thirsty man the milk of the senses. He let the placidity of *The Milkmaid* flow into him. Her humble room with the broken pane of glass and pitted wall and broken bread round. The dignity and importance of her action, the pouring of milk, so real he could almost hear it splash into the brown earthenware bowl. Yes. And he'd gotten the folds of her sleeve right not just by altering color tones as every painter did, but by varying the thickness of paint. The day he discovered that, he knew it would change the way he painted fabric forever. It was just days after a child was born, Francis maybe, or Beatrix, and he was bursting with wild excitement from a marvel so separate he couldn't share it with Catharina. That discovery alone should convince him to continue now, but it did not. Now, plunged into the melancholy of being between paintings, and feverish with longing for the moment when the next would reveal itself to him, he admitted: It did not convince.

Later that afternoon he walked back through a neighborhood of open workshops near the Oostyende Canal, heading for something, he felt, though what it was remained unclear to him. He passed a tallow candlemaker dipping a row of hanging wicks in a steaming vat. He passed a saddler, a blacksmith, a furniture maker; a fuller felting cloth in a wooden trough; a carver gouging wood behind rows of *klompen* and clocks, wooden bowls and spoons; a faience painter applying the same blue windmill, the same willow tree to stacks of plates. All apparently content at their anvils or tubs or benches. He felt no affinity with any of them.

He thought of his father years ago, leaning forward, lifting the silk warp threads with the tip of his shuttle to reproduce the fine patterns of his drawings in the damasked cloth. Had it given him any satisfaction?

The quick beat of wooden clogs on paving stones rang out from around a corner. Before he could stop, a young girl collided with him, her skirts flying. It was his second eldest daughter.

"Magdalena!"

"Father!"

"Where are you going in such an

unwholesome hurry?" He smoothed her hair.

"To the town walls," she said breathlessly. "Mother said I could. I've got my chores done and you weren't there to keep the little ones quiet for. I'll be home soon. It's just to look."

"I know. I know how you love it." Her light brown hair fell unbraided — she'd left home without a cap — and in the breeze, her lifted hair backlit, she appeared ethereal.

"Come with me, Father. Oh, please. What you can see from there!" Her whole body quivered with the anticipation of it.

He chuckled at her urgency and shook his head. He'd already played nine pins with his boys in the lane that morning because they had begged him, said he'd promised, and he had. But it was already late in the afternoon and he had to get on with this. "I will someday. Mind you be home before sunset." As she turned he noticed the heels of her clogs worn down to thin uneven plates.

The way she'd asked, brimming over with enthusiasm and hope, was just the way she'd asked last winter for him to take her ice sailing and he had said no, and that week the weather turned unseasonably warm and broke up the ice and they missed their chance. He'd felt wounded and bereft. He lived so badly, it seemed, because he always came into the moment encumbered. He almost had a mind to turn around and catch up to her, but he walked on, taking a circuitous route in order to pass under the dappled leafiness of the lime trees lining the canals.

He avoided the market square because he owed Hendrick a bread bill. The day before, Hendrick's reminder of the amount shocked him, four hundred eighty guilders. More than a year's pay for one of those craftsmen. And there were other debts to the grocer and woolener. And now, those worn shoes sent him further into an abyss of despondency.

By some thread pulling him along, he found himself on Mols Laen. He paused at his cousin's house and shop, was relieved to find him not present, then crossed the peat market quickly to the Papists' Corner on the Oude Langendijck where his mother-in-law lived, the aristocratic matron, Maria Thins. Before her waxed oaken door, he thought of Magdalena's worn clogs, and then lifted the silver knocker. He asked, straight away, with no softening cordial prelude: Could she advance him two hundred guilders against the sale of his next painting?

She focused her eyes past him, over his shoulder as if some inanimate thing behind him, a crack in the wall or the decorated virginal, were of more pressing interest. It was her way of making him feel like a beggar even though she owed him plenty, though it wasn't money. On many occasions he'd saved her witless son Willem from the magistrates when he made a spectacle of himself in the market square. More than once Willem had lowered his drawers and bent over, cackling at Catharina, Willem's own sister, when she'd encountered him there. And he, Jan, had had to intervene countless times to stop a brawl in The Mechelen, his mother's tavern next door, and usually, Willem was at the bottom of it. In spite of this, Maria Thins made him feel unworthy. Still, he looked her in the face. Even at home she was wearing rubies in her stretched white earlobes.

"I'm getting known in Delft now," he said.

"By whom? One brewer? One baker? Any commissions? No. Any church panels?"

"Of course not. Dutch Reformed

churches do not hire painters who've converted to Papists."

He saw the slight pulling back of her chin, which showed its fleshy under-twin. It was she who had demanded his conversion, including confirmation by the bishop, as a condition of his marrying Catharina, and he'd been willing despite its possible effects on his career.

"I've been elected as headman of the Guild of St. Luke," he said.

"So I've heard. Congratulations. Does it pay?" The thin bones in the back of her hand rose and fell as she drummed her jeweled fingers on the tapestry draping the table before her.

"A little. Something else might come of it."

"Might. Might. Meanwhile Catharina is with child."

"Unless that son of yours scared it out of her. He chased her with a stick across the market square last week. She doesn't go out now."

"I'm sorry, Jan. Willem's always been unruly, always jealous."

"It's gone far beyond jealousy. The man is dangerous, if not to others, then to himself. How can you defend him when he's attacked you too?"

She rubbed the skin of her temple, as if pushing against memory. "What can I do? He learned it from his father."

"What can *I* do?"

"If you wanted your family to have better than a few rusks for breakfast, you'd give up painting. You'd hire out to one of the potteries. Surely now with your new status in the guild, some pottery will take you on as a faience painter. You can still turn your brushwork into guilders. Into potatoes and *hutspot* and bread. Into blankets and boots for your boys," she went on.

Plate after relentless plate. He imagined them stacked in a wall before him. His knees weakened and he looked away, at the things in the room. He often felt profoundly moved by the expressive power of objects in a room. A golden water pitcher sitting on a narrow red-patterned cloth as if on an altar reflected a dozen shades from scarlet to yellow-gold. He liked the straight, strong lines rising from the solid base and the voluptuous curve of the handle.

"That's a handsome pitcher," he said. "Do you have another one you could use just for a while? I like the way the cloth is reflected in the gold. Maybe I could paint —"

"Take it. Take it. The cloth too." She waved it away, and he felt he'd been waved away too. "Why God gave me such a son-in-law. Son and son-in-law, both irresponsible. Both crazed."

"The advance?"

"I'll think on it. I can't promise. Willem gets furious if he thinks I'm favoring you, and then he breaks things. He hasn't forgotten the last loan. And he thinks I'll give a sizable endowment at the christening. But I can't. Rents due me from the Beijerlands are in arrears."

"I thought if only I could have enough to rent a small studio then I'd have no interruptions and I could produce more."

"I said I'll think on it."

On the way home carrying the pitcher wrapped in the cloth, he felt a sick, hollow ache descending with nightfall. He'd have to face Catharina without a stuiver. He'd tell her tonight he would work at something else. A disgrace to ask at a pottery. He'd never be regarded as an artisan after that. Only a craftsman. Better to do something entirely different. He'd work for his cousin selling cloth. He'd start tomorrow. For only a couple years. Maybe less if he did well. To interrupt what little continuity he had would be disastrous to his work. It would be a long crawl back.

He heard shouting when he was still a few houses away. Neighbors gathered in front of his door. He ran inside. In the main room he found his children screaming, Geertruida and the baby crying, and Willem beating Catharina with a stick. She had fallen onto her spinning wheel and curled there on the floor against it trying to protect her unborn child. With a furious swing, Jan struck him on the head with the base of the pitcher. It stunned him enough that Jan could pull him off Catharina and deliver a mighty blow to his stomach. Willem fell, crushing an easel. Jan kicked him and yanked his arms behind him and sat on him.

"Francis, fetch me some twine. All we've got. Maria, Cornelia, tend to your mother." While Willem was still dazed, Jan bound him, hand and foot, to a straight-backed chair, and tied the chair to the stairway. Then he saw the stick. An iron pin protruded from its end. "Johannes, roust out van Overgaeu, the man who set your arm. Remember? Four houses down. Toward the church. Where is that Magdalena? Beatrix, fetch your Grandmother Maria. Carry a lantern, child. It's getting dark."

The room spun upon the point of the

iron pin until he heard his wife whisper to the older girls, "I'm all right. I'm all right," already diminishing it for the children's sake. He was, after all, their uncle, she'd say. Jan took the wet cloth from his eldest daughter and washed Catharina's arm where the nail had left a long, deep scratch.

"How did it begin?"

"He came in raving."

Willem stirred and began to shout something wild about a she-devil. Jan gagged him with the red cloth and came back to Catharina filled with self-reproach for his own negligence. If he had been home, this wouldn't have happened. Swallowing back remorse, he stroked Catharina's face and throat with the damp cloth.

"I'm all right," she said.

"But the child."

Foreign, disturbed air filled the room all the way into the corners. The Spanish chair overturned, the spinning wheel broken, his painting of *Christ in the House of Mary and Martha* hanging crooked, the tablecloth pulled off the table, earthenware bowls broken on the floor, the children's soup spilled, the wooden cradle rocking and its forgotten occupant still crying unattended — all order in his universe disarranged. The cradle still rocking from having been knocked in the scuffle made a rhythmic crackling sound. The town scene he'd painted on the side of the cradle, practice for his *View of Delft*, caught the light, then didn't, then did. It was a long moment before he stepped over to bring it to rest. The cradle had survived longer than the baby it was made for, his grandmother, a fact that struck him now with wonder. How things can live longer than people.

He lifted the baby to his shoulder, the down of infant's hair heavenly soft against his own cheek. Swaying from side to side, soothing her, he breathed the child's sweet, milky smell, felt her little mouth trying to suckle his neck.

Van Overgeau came immediately to examine Catharina and dress the wound, but Maria Thins kept Jan waiting a sufficient amount of time to communicate without a doubt that she wouldn't be hurried. The moment she arrived, her eyes showing too much white, she swept over to Catharina's bedside.

"I'm all right, Mother."

Jan put it to Maria Thins directly. "I can summon the magistrates and have him clapped in prison, or we can confine him ourselves in a private house of correction."

Her nostrils flared, her eyes darted about uncontrollably. "Where?"

"Taerling's."

Willem squirmed violently against the twine across his chest, and tried to speak.

She hesitated. Jan held up the stick with the iron pin to show her. "It's better than a public asylum."

Alarm shot out from her eyes. In one instant, obligation shifted. She was incurring a huge debt to him. Tearfully, unable to look at her son gagged and moaning, she nodded agreement. Before she could change her mind, Jan asked a neighbor to fetch Taerling. "And have him bring manacles."

Jan and Catharina passed the night in mute shock. The next day, she lost the new baby. Jan sat with Catharina every day until she recovered. Feeling helpless, he brought her broth in a cup, and mended her spinning wheel. And every night for a week, he lurched awake at Geertruida's shrieks, held her hot, damp body, sobbing from her nightmare, until warm milk and his arms around her calmed her enough for her to sleep again.

Too soon the other children resumed

their boisterous play and argument. Doors banged. Children outside wanted in. Children inside wanted out. The two youngest boys, Francis and Ignatius, took to imitating what they'd seen, and staged fights knocking heads with wooden mugs, kicking bellies, tying up the vanquished. They squabbled over who would be Papa and who would be Uncle Willem, the mug yanked back and forth between them until the fighting was real. Jan stormed at them to stop.

He agreed to oversee Willem's confinement in the house of correction. Being his brother's keeper seemed a spurious way to gain entrance into the Kingdom of Heaven. Couldn't he paint his way in instead? He felt his life slipping.

Maria Thins lent him three hundred guilders. It wasn't the same as earning money from his art, but it gave him some time. He paid enough to appease the baker and the grocer, bought the children new shoes, made a payment on the iceboat, and bought bricks of pigment and Venetian turpentine. Then it was gone.

If only he could work faster. Paint, Johannes, paint, he told himself. Yet if he did work faster, how could he produce paintings grounded in deep beds of contemplation, the only way living things could be stilled long enough to understand them? And wasn't everything he painted — a breadbasket, a pitcher, a jewelry box, a copper pail — wasn't it all living?

Pulverizing a small brick of ultramarine with a mortar and pestle one day, loving the intensity of blue as rich as powdered lapis lazuli, he heard a commotion in the main room. His second daughter. Magdalena. Far too old for this. As soon as he entered, she stopped shouting. Fear of making a move stilled everyone, even Ignatius. Blessed silence, marred by the scrape of her chair against the tile floor when she backed away from him.

In a moment she lifted her face to his, her cheeks rosy with shame. Regret glazing her eyes softened him. She stood before him as if offered by God. The blue cloth of her smock draped like billowy sky. There was something in this girl he could never grasp, an inner life inscrutable to him. He was in awe of the child's flights of fancy, her insatiable passion always to be running off somewhere, her active inner life. To still it for a moment, long enough to paint, for eternity, ah.

Was it possible to paint with good conscience what he didn't understand? What he didn't even know?

"Sit down."

Painting was the only way even to attempt to know it.

The chair scraped again when she moved to sit at the corner table by the window.

Her eyes, pale cerulean. How had he never noticed? The face, not beautiful; the expression charged yet under containment — for him, he believed. To render it with honesty rather than pride or even mere love, to go beyond the painting of known sentiments into mystery — that was her challenge to him. His sense of obligation deepened, renewed itself, as Pieter had said. The open window reflected her face, and in one pane, the image of her cheek shone luminous as though blended with the dust of crushed pearls. He opened the window a few centimeters more, then less, settling on an angle. A whiff of breeze stirred the loose hair at her temple.

"If you sit here, I will paint you, Magdalena. But only if you stop that shouting." Her eyes opened wider and she pursed her lips shut against the smile that might burst into words. He brought the sewing basket, placed it on the table, and thought of its dear, humble history, picked out by Catharina from a dozen at some merchant's stall. He moved Geertruida's glass of milk into the slant of light, that glass that someone had washed the day before and the day before that. He set the golden pitcher near it and slightly behind. It shimmered in the stream of sunlight, reflecting blue from Magdalena's sleeve. No. He took it away. It was beautiful, but there was more truth without it. He placed on Magdalena's lap her brother's shirt that needed buttons. He adjusted her shoulders, and felt them tighten, then slowly relax under his hands. He arranged her skirt and her white linen cap Catharina had made. Her hand had fallen palm upward on the shirt, her delicate fingers curled. Perfect. It was not in the act of doing anything. Any intended action was forgotten and therefore it was full of peace.

In a sudden movement his wife rushed over to take away Geertruida's glass of milk.

"No, leave it, Catharina. Right there in the light. It makes the whole corner sacred with the tenderness of just living."

In the arranging of these things he felt a pleasure his selfishness surely didn't deserve. He stepped back and breathed more slowly, and what he saw, lit by warming washes of honey and gold, was a respite in stillness from the unacknowledged acts of women to hallow home. That stillness today, he thought, might be all he would ever know of the Kingdom of Heaven.

Magdalena Looking

Late one afternoon when Magdalena finished the clothes washing and her mother let her go out, she ran from their house by the Nieuwe Kerk across the market square, past van Buyten's bakery, over two cobbled bridges across the canals, past the blacksmith's all the way to Kethelstraat and the town wall where she climbed up and up the ochre stone steps, each one as high as her knee, to her favorite spot in all of Delft, the round sentry post. From that great height, oh, what she could see. If only she could paint it. In one direction Schiedam Gate and beyond it the twin towers of Rotterdam Gate, and ships with odd-shaped sails the color of brown eggshells coming up the great Schie River from the sea, and in another direction strips of potato fields with wooden plows casting shadows over the soil like long fingers, and orchards, rows of rounded green as ordered as Mother wished their eleven young lives to be, and the smoke of the potteries and brickeries, and beyond that, she didn't know. She didn't know.

She stood there looking, looking, and behind her she heard the creak and thrum of the south windmill turning like her heart in the sea wind, and she breathed the brine that had washed here from other shores. Below her the Schie lay like a pale yellow ribbon along the town wall. The longer she looked, the more it seemed to borrow its color from the sky. In the wind, the boats along the Schie docks with their fasteners clanking and their hollow bellies nudging one another made a kind of low rattling music she loved. It wasn't just today. She loved the sentry post in every kind of weather. To see rain pocking the gray sea and shimmering the stone bridge, to feel its cold strings of water on her face and hands, filled her to bursting.

She moved to a notch in the wall and just then a gust of wind lifted her skirts. The men on the bridge waiting with their bundles to go to sea shouted something in words she did not understand. She'd never tell Mother. Mother did not want her going there. The sentry post was full of guards smoking tobacco, Mother had said. There was some dark thing in her voice, as though she thought Magdalena should be afraid, but Magdalena did not know how to feel that then, or there.

Up there, high up above the town, she had longings no one in the family knew. No one would ever know them, she thought, unless perhaps a soul would read her face or she herself would have soul enough to speak of them. Wishes had the power to knock the breath out of her. Some were large and throbbing and persistent, some mere pinpricks of golden light, short-lived as fireflies but keenly felt. She wished for her chores to be done so she'd have time to race to the town wall every day before supper, or to the Oude Kerk to lift the fallen leaves from her brother's grave. She wished her baby sisters wouldn't cry so, and the boys wouldn't quarrel and wrestle underfoot or run shouting through the house. Father wished that too, she knew. She wished there were not so many bowls to wash, thirteen each meal. She wished her hair shone flaxen in the sunlight of the market square like little Geertruida's. She wished she could travel in a carriage across borders to all the lands drawn on her father's map.

She wished the grocer wouldn't treat her so gruffly when he saw her hand open out to offer four guilders, all that her mother gave her to pay the grocery bill that was mounting into the hundreds, as far as she could tell. She wished he wouldn't shout; it sent his garlic breath straight into her nostrils. The baker, Hendrick van Buyten, was kinder. Two times so far he let Father pay with a painting so they could start over. Sometimes he gave her a still-warm bun to eat while walking home. And sometimes he put a curl of honey on it. She wished the grocer was like him.

She wished Father would take the iceboat to the Schie more often. He'd bought a fine one with a tall ivory sail. "Eighty guilders," Mother grumbled. "Better a winter's worth of bread and meat." On winter Sundays if the weather was clear, and if he was between paintings, it whisked them skimming across the white glass of the canal. She'd never known such speed. The sharp cold air blew life and hope and excitement into her ears and open mouth.

She remembered wishing, one particular morning when Father mixed lead white with the smallest dot of lead-tin yellow for the goose quill in a painting of Mother writing a letter, that she might someday have someone to write to, that she could write at the end of a letter full of love and news, "As ever, your loving Magdalena Elisabeth."

He painted Mother often, and Maria he painted once, draped her head in a golden mantle and her shoulders in a white satin shawl. She was older, fifteen, though only by eleven months. It might be fun to dress up like Maria did, and wear pearl earrings and have Father position her just so, but the only part she really wished for was that he would look and look and pay attention.

More than all those wishes, she had one pulsing wish that outshone all the others. She wished to paint. Yes, me, she thought, leaning out over the stone wall. I want to paint. This and everything. The world from that vantage point stretched so grandly. Up there, beauty was more than color and shapes, but openness, light, the air itself, and because of that, it seemed untouchable. If only the act of wishing would make her able. Father only smiled queerly when she told him she wanted to paint, just as if she'd said she wanted to sail the seas, which, of course, she also wished, in order to paint what she would see. When she said so, that she wished to paint, Mother thrust into her hands the basket of mending to do.

Often from the edge of the room, she'd

watch him work. Because he was always asking for quiet, with the little ones running through the room laughing or shouting, she didn't ask him many questions. He rarely answered anyway. Still, she studied how much linseed oil he used to thin the ultramarine, and watched him apply it over a glassy layer of reddish brown. By magic, it made the dress he painted warmer than the blue on the palette. He would not let her go with him to the attic where he ground lead-tin yellow to powder, but he did send her to the apothecary for the small bricks of it, and for linseed oil. Always there was money for that, but she didn't know what to answer when the apothecary demanded the guilders for her brother's potions still owed after he died.

If only she could have colors of her own, and brushes. She wouldn't just paint pictures of women inside cramped little rooms. She'd paint them out in marketplaces, bending in the potato fields, talking in doorways in the sunlight, in boats on the Schie, or praying in the Oude Kerk. Or she'd paint people skating, fathers teaching their children on the frozen Schie.

Fathers teaching their children. The thought stopped her.

Looking from the sentry tower at a cloud darkening the river, she knew, just as she knew she'd always have washing and mending to do, that it would not be so. She'd worn herself out with wishing, and turned to go. She had to be home to help with supper.

On a spring day that began in no special way, except that she had climbed the town wall the afternoon before, and all over Delft lime trees lining the canals had burst into chartreuse leaves, and light shone through them and made them yellower except where one leaf crossed over another and so was darker — on that spring-certain day, out of some unknown, unborn place came that scream. "I hate to mend," she shouted to the walls, to Mother, to anyone. "It's not making anything."

Father stepped into the room, looked at Mother and then scowled at Magdalena. It had been her job to keep her little brothers quiet for him, or shoo them out of doors, and here she was, the noisy one. No one moved. Even the boys were still. At first she looked only at Father's hand smeared with ultramarine powder, not in his eyes, too surprised by the echo of her voice to fling out any additional defiance. She loved him, loved what he did with that hand, and even, she suspected, loved what he loved, though they had not spoken of it. When that thought lifted her face to his, she saw his cheeks grow softer, as if he noticed her in his house for the first time. He drew her over to the table by the window, brought the sewing basket, placed on her lap her brother's shirt that needed buttons, adjusted the chair, opened the window, a little more, then less, and discovered that at a certain angle, it reflected her face. "If you sit here mending, I will paint you, Magdalena. But only if you stop that shouting." He positioned her shoulders, and his hands resting a moment were warm through the muslin of her smock and seemed to settle her.

Mother rushed over to take away Geertruida's glass of milk.

"No, leave it, Catharina. Right there in the light."

For days she sat there, still as she could for Father, and yet sewing a few stitches every so often to satisfy Mother. In that mood of stillness, all the things within her line of vision touched her deeply. The tapestry laid across the table, the sewing basket, the same glass repoured each day to the same level, the amber-toned map of the world on the wall — it plucked a lute

218

string in her heart that these things she'd touched, grown as familiar to her as her own skin, would be looked at, marveled at, maybe even loved by viewers of his painting.

On sunny days the panes of window glass glistened before her. Like jewels melted into flat squares, she thought. Each one was slightly different in its pale transparent color — ivory, parchment, the lightest of wines and the palest of tulips. She wondered how glass was made, but she didn't ask. It would disturb him.

Outside the window the market chattered with the selling of apples and lard and brooms and wooden buckets. She liked the cheese porters in their flat-brimmed red hats and stark white clothes. Their curved yellow carrying platforms stacked neatly with cheese rounds were suspended on ropes between pairs of them, casting brown shadows on the paving stones. Two platforms diagonally placed in the midground between their carriers would make a nice composition with the repeated shapes of those bulging cheese rounds. She'd put a delivery boy wheeling his cart of silver cod in the background against the guild hall, and maybe in the foreground a couple of lavender gray pigeons pecking crumbs. The carillon from Nieuwe Kerk ringing out the hour sounded something profound in her chest. All of it is ordinary to everyone but me, she thought.

All that month she did not speak, the occasion too momentous to dislodge it with words. He said he'd paint her as long as she didn't shout, and so she did not speak a word. Her chest ached like a dull wound when she realized that her silence did not cause him a moment's reflection or curiosity. When she looked out the corner of her eye at him, she could not tell what she meant to him. Slowly, she came to understand that he looked at her with the same interest he gave to the glass of milk.

Maybe it was because she wasn't pretty like Maria. She knew her jaws protruded and her watery, pale eyes were too widely set. She had a mole on her forehead that she always tried to hide by tugging at her cap. What if no one would want the painting? What then? It might be her fault, because she wasn't pretty. She wished he'd say something about her, but all he said, not to her directly, more to himself, was how the sunlight whitened her cap at the forehead, how the shadow at the nape of her neck reflected blue from her collar, or how the sienna of her skirt deepened to Venetian red in the folds. It was never her, she cried to herself, only something surrounding her that she did not make or even contribute to knowingly. Another wish that never would come true, she saw then, even if she lived forever, was that he, that someone, would look at her not as an artistic study, but with love. If two people love the same thing, she reasoned, then they must love each other, at least a little, even if they never say it. Nevertheless, because he painted with such studied concentration, and because she held him in awe, she practiced looking calm for him as she looked out the window, but when she saw the canvas, what she intended as calm looked more like wistfulness.

The painting was not bought by the brewer, Pieter Claesz van Ruijven, who bought most of her father's work. He saw it, but passed over it for another. Disgrace seared her so that she could not speak that night. The painting hung without a frame in the outer kitchen where the younger children slept. Eventually the family had to give up their lodgings at Mechelen on the square, and take smaller rooms with Grandmother Maria on the Oude Langendijck. Her father stopped taking the ice-boat out to the Schie, sold it, in fact. He rarely painted, the rooms were so cramped and dark, the younger children boisterous, and a few years later, he died.

When she washed him in his bed that last time, his fingers already cold, she had a thought, the shame of which prevented her from uttering: It would make a fine painting, a memorial, the daughter with towel and blue-figured washing bowl at bedside, her hand covering his, the wife exhausted on the Spanish chair clutching a crucifix, the father-husband, eyes glazed, looking to another landscape. While he painted everyone else, no one was there to paint him, to make him remembered. She yearned to do it, but the task was too fearsome. She lacked the skill, and the one to teach her had never offered.

Even though she asked for them, Mother sold his paints and brushes to the Guild of St. Luke. It helped to pay a debt. When Mother became sick with worry, Magdalena had the idea to take the painting to Hendrick van Buyten, the baker, because she knew he liked her. And he accepted it, along with one of a lady playing a guitar, for the debt of six hundred seventeen guilders, six stuivers, more than two years' worth of bread. He smiled at her and gave her a bun.

Within a year, she married a saddlemaker named Nicolaes, the first man to notice her, a hard worker whose pores smelled of leather and grease, who taught her a pleasure not of the eyes, but, she soon realized, a man utterly without imagination. They moved to Amsterdam and she didn't see the painting again for twenty years.

In 1696, just after their only living child, Magritte, damp with fever, stopped breathing in her arms, Magdalena read in the Amsterdamsche Courant of a public auction of one hundred thirty-four paintings by various artists. "Several outstandingly artful paintings," the notice said, "including twenty-one works most powerfully and splendidly painted by the late J. Vermeer of Delft, will be auctioned May 16, 1:00, at the Oude Heeren Logement." Only a week away. She thought of Hendrick. Of course he couldn't be expected to keep those paintings forever. Hers might be there. The possibility kept her awake nights.

Entering the auction gallery, she was struck again by that keenest of childhood wishes — to make a record not only of what she saw, but how. The distance she'd come from that, and not even a child to show for it! She shocked herself by asking, involuntarily, what had been the point of having lived? Wishing had not been enough. Was it a mistake that she didn't beg him to teach her? Maybe not. If she'd seen that eventually, with help, she could paint, it might have made the years of birthing and dying harder. But then the birthing and dying would have been painted and the pain given. It would have served a purpose. Would that have been enough — to tell a truth in art?

She didn't know.

To see again so many of Father's paintings was like walking down an avenue of her childhood. The honey-colored window, the Spanish chair, the map she'd stared at, dreaming, hanging on the wall, Grandmother Maria's golden water pitcher, Mother's pearls and yellow satin jacket — they commanded such a reverence for her now that she felt they all had souls.

And suddenly there she was on canvas, framed. Her knees went weak.

Hendrick hadn't kept it. Even though he liked her, he hadn't kept it.

Almost a child she was, it seemed to her, gazing out the window instead of doing her mending, as if by the mere act of looking she could send her spirit out into the world. And those shoes! She had forgotten. How she loved the buckles, and thought they made her such a lady. Eventually she'd worn the soles right through, but now, brand-new, the buckles glinted on the canvas, each with a point of golden light. A bubble of joy surged upward right through her.

No, she wasn't beautiful, she owned, but there was a simplicity in her young face that she knew the years had eroded, a stilled longing in the forward lean of her body, a wishing in the intensity of her eyes. The painting showed she did not yet know that lives end abruptly, that much of living is repetition and separation, that buttons forever need re-sewing no matter how ferociously one works the thread, that nice things almost happen. Still a woman overcome with wishes, she wished Nicolaes would have come with her to see her in the days of her sentry post wonder when life and hope were new and full of possibility, but he had seen no reason to close up the shop on such a whim.

She stood on tiptoe and didn't breathe when her painting was announced. Her hand in her pocket closed tight around the twenty-four guilders, some of it borrowed from two neighbor women, some of it taken secretly from the box where Nicolaes kept money for leather supplies. It was all she could find, and she didn't dare ask for more. He would have thought it foolish.

"Twenty," said a man in front of her.

"Twenty-two," said another.

"Twenty-four," she said so loud and fast the auctioneer was startled. Did he see something similar in her face? He didn't call for another bid. The painting was hers!

"Twenty-five."

Her heart cracked.

The rest was a blur of sound. It finally went to a man who kept conferring with his wife, which she took as a good sign that it was going to a nice family. Forty-seven guilders. Most of the paintings sold for much more, but forty-seven was fine, she thought. In fact, it filled her momentarily with what she'd been taught was the sin of pride. Then she thought of Hendrick and a pain lashed through her. Forty-seven guilders minus the auctioneer's fee didn't come close to what her family had owed him.

She followed the couple out into the drizzle of Herengracht, wanting to make herself known to them, just to have a few words, but then dropped back. She had such bad teeth now, and they were people of means. The woman wore stockings. What would she say to them? She didn't want them to think she wanted anything.

She walked away slowly along a wet stone wall that shone iridescent, and the wetness of the street reflected back the blue of her best dress. Water spots appeared fast, turning the cerulean to deep ultramarine, Father's favorite blue. Light rain pricked the charcoal green canal water into delicate, dark lace, and she wondered if it had ever been painted just that way, or if the life of something as inconsequential as a water drop could be arrested and given to the world in a painting, or if the world would care.

She thought of all the people in all the paintings she had seen that day, not just Father's, in all the paintings of the world, in fact. Their eyes, the particular turn of a head, their loneliness or suffering or grief was borrowed by an artist to be seen by other people throughout the years who would never see them face to face. People who would be that close to her, she thought, a matter of a few arms' lengths, looking, looking, and they would never know her.

The employees of Thorndike Press hope you have enjoyed this Large Print book. All our Large Print titles are designed for easy reading, and all our books are made to last. Other Thorndike Press Large Print books are available at your library, through selected bookstores, or directly from us.

For information about titles, please call:

(800) 257-5157

To share your comments, please write:

Publisher
Thorndike Press
P.O. Box 159
Thorndike, Maine 04986